Christmastime 1944

A Love Story

LINDA MAHKOVEC

Other Books by Linda Mahkovec

The Dreams of Youth

Seven Tales of Love

The Garden House

The Christmastime Series

Christmastime 1939: Prequel
to The Christmastime Series

Christmastime 1940: A Love Story

Christmastime 1941: A Love Story

Christmastime 1942: A Love Story

Christmastime 1943: A Love Story

Christmastime 1945: A Love Story

Christmastime 1944: A Love Story
by Linda Mahkovec

...

Copyright © 2017

ISBN-10: 1-946229-69-5
ISBN-13: 978-1-946229-69-4

Distributed by Bublish, Inc.

Cover Design by Laura Duffy
© Nick Martucci/Shutterstock.com

To my brothers, Bill and Andy –
Many thanks.

Historical note:
In WWII, there were over 425,000 prisoners of war (mostly German) in the United States, with POW camps in all but four states. They were used to help fill the labor shortage, working on farms, and in canneries and factories.

Chapter 1

The newspaper headlines, radio bulletins, and movie newsreels of 1944 surged with war updates from faraway places. The Allied advance across the Pacific: Saipan, the Philippine Sea, Leyte Gulf. The taking back of Europe: Anzio, Monte Cassino, the beaches of Normandy. 1944 was a mix of victory, triumph, and euphoria – alongside destruction, defeat, and despair.

In the Pacific, there were decisive naval victories – and, less talked about, gruesome hand-to-hand combat on the islands, and the beginning of kamikaze attacks. In Europe, there was the triumphant march through Paris – on the heels of the slaughter at Omaha Beach. There was the liberation of the first concentration camp – and the horrors revealed within. The human spirit soared at countless acts of heroism and sacrifice – and sickened at what it was capable of. After six tumultuous years, the direction of the war was finally pointing to an Allied victory. It was, at long last, the beginning of the end.

It was December, and in New York City, a freezing rain seemed to symbolize the coldness that gripped the heart of the world. On the street, and in the office buildings and apartment buildings, weariness and hope competed for dominance.

And yet, beneath the rain and ice, the first signs of Christmas could now be seen, bolstering the side of hope. The side of family and tradition and happiness. Pine wreaths and red ribbons hung in windows and on doors, strings of colored lights brightened the store awnings and window displays – as well as the booths for war bonds, Red Cross blood drives, and the recruiting stations.

Inside Rockwell Publishing, the offices buzzed and bustled, phones rang, and employees hurried to meetings and pushed themselves to meet deadlines. In the Art Department, Mr. Rockwell himself hammered home his expectations for the numerous campaigns and deadlines. He gathered up his papers and slammed shut his folder, signaling that the meeting was over.

But Lillian Drooms stubbornly continued her defense. "Mr. Rockwell, I don't think you realize – "

"We've got deadlines and this is no time for arguments," Rockwell said, scowling for emphasis. "I've been in this business a helluva lot longer than you. I know what works."

"Yes, Mr. Rockwell. Of course. I simply meant to suggest that – "

"When I want your opinion, Mrs. Drooms, I'll ask for it. Until then, do as I say!" He pushed off from the table and rose to his feet.

Mr. Brache, the head of Art, tried to catch Lillian's eye, making small gestures with his hands that said – *no more, please!*

Lillian pressed her lips together, took her drawings, and followed Mr. Rockwell as he made his way through the Art Department. Though he rarely visited this part of his publishing empire, he periodically called a meeting to whip up the pace and urgency of production. When he did so, the effect was that of a small storm swirling through the office. Folders and portfolios were immediately opened and drawings spread out, workers bumped into one another and dropped papers as they hastened back to their desks, everyone in a hurry to respond to his demands – until he was out of the office. Then they would sigh in relief and for the most part, work got back on schedule after the disruption.

But Lillian had worked for the past two weeks on her *Glamour in Wartime* campaign and was confident in her drawings. Mr. Rockwell was simply missing the point.

He saw her on his heels, which was enough to provoke his ire. If there was one thing he couldn't tolerate it was disagreement with his ideas.

He tried to ignore her persistence by continuing with his argument, waving his unlit cigar and chopping the air for emphasis. "How is it you always have an opinion about everything anymore? Always second guessing my decisions, always wanting to change a hairstyle here, a dress there. And now it's age!"

"But Mr. Rockwell, with so many women *of all ages* in the workforce now, it just doesn't make sense to depict them all as 'young and bouncy' as you say, when in fact – "

He spun around. "Young and bouncy sells soap!" He held up his hand as Lillian began to argue her point. "End of discussion. You've let that campaign over the summer go to your head! Your expertise on a weed is one thing, but this is an entirely different matter."

Lillian's mouth dropped open. "If you're referring to the milkweed campaign – "

"Where's my assistant?" He scanned the room. "Miss Briggs!" Rockwell turned to his left, then his right. "Izzy!" In trying to locate Izzy and dodge Lillian, he found himself back at the conference table.

Izzy remained seated and exchanged a glance of understanding with her friend Lillian, accompanied by a slow shake of her head. She took a deep breath before replying.

"Yes? Mr. Rockwell?" she answered, each word weighted with effort.

"Over here! Can't you see I'm ready to leave? Call Seaton's again and demand that they send those figures immediately."

Izzy raised herself. "I already called them this morni- "

"Then call them again! And bring the current report to Mr. Brache. And I want that position in Production filled by the end of this week. No more delays." Rockwell continued out into the hall where one of his minions held the elevator door open for him.

His last demand roused Izzy and she hurried to catch up with him as he entered the elevator. "Mr. Rockwell, I told you that position has already been filled."

"And I told *you* Mr. Casey is not up to the task. I want – "

His voice faded as the elevator door closed on their discussion.

Lillian blew out a sigh of relief. Poor Izzy, she thought. At least Rockwell's visits to the Art Department were limited. Izzy, as Mr. Rockwell's office manager, had him shadowing her all day long.

Lillian stood at her desk, flipping through the drawings of female workers she had so passionately worked on. They meant a lot to her. She had faithfully captured the spirit and determination of the older female train conductor, the white-haired postal clerk, the grandmother running a recycling center. She sat down and rested her chin in her hand, tapping her pencil in frustration.

One of her colleagues, a young woman whose husband had been killed on D-Day, walked by and gently touched her shoulder. "Give him what he wants," she said. "It's just soap, after all."

Lillian watched the woman sit at her desk and continue her work on the Sixth War Bonds' campaign. The poor woman had three small children and was struggling, barely holding it together. Lillian had heard that she was seeing a much older man. Not much romance involved, to be sure, but with three children and her spirit crushed, it seemed a solution of sorts. Everyone was desperate and exhausted, clinging to their jobs, their families, to any idea that offered a glimmer of normalcy.

Glancing around the office, Lillian observed the other artists. A soldier who had come back a year ago and still jumped at the smallest sound. The heartbroken young girls who had lost their fiancés. A father whose two sons had died in the Pacific. The list went on.

She took a deep breath and studied the women in the soap ads. She would redraw them as young and hopeful – women whose lives had not yet been shattered by war. She would depict them as charming, fresh, and lovely. Full of a happy future.

An hour later, Izzy returned with the report for Mr. Brache. She stopped by Lillian's desk, her face flushed with anger.

Lillian raised her head. "What is it?"

"He's trying to prevent me from rehiring Mr. Casey," Izzy said, folding her arms. "The man worked here for ten years! He comes back wounded, and Rockwell doesn't have the decency to give him his job back. The poor man goes to war, leaves his family, does his duty – something Rockwell didn't have the guts to do, which I pointed out to him – "

"Oh, Izzy, you didn't!" Lillian worried about Izzy's increasing antagonism with their boss. She was growing more and more outspoken and defiant. "You told me that Mr. Casey had already quit on his own when the war broke out – "

"Because Rockwell drove him to it. I was there and remember how Rockwell used to hound him! Anyway, today I insisted that Mr. Casey have his old job back. With an increase in salary."

Lillian's eyes widened at her friend's boldness.

"I convinced him that it was the patriotic thing to do. That it would boost morale and make him look good."

"That's all true. Did he agree?"

"He said he would think about it. But he told me I was skating on thin ice and that his patience with me was running out. *His* patience with *me*? Ha!"

Izzy tilted her head to examine Lillian's new sketch and smiled at the pretty woman choosing a bar of soap. Young, lovely, casting her eyes up shyly at a soldier in uniform.

"I don't know how you do it, Lilly. In that one glance, I see a romance, an end of the war, babies, and a cozy home. That's why the brute pushes you. You always come up with something like this. It makes me happy to think that such a sweet young couple is out there – just beginning their lives." She grinned at Lillian. "What's the brand of that soap? I think I'll buy myself a bar."

Lillian looked down at the drawing. "I guess Mr. Rockwell was right."

"Right about the soap. Wrong about Mr. Casey!" Izzy said, thumping her fist on the desk. She gave out a long, anguished groan. "And tomorrow is the dinner event *honoring* Rockwell. Which means he donated a chunk of money. Oh, I'm going to have to be nice to him all evening – it'll kill me,

Lilly. It'll kill me. I'll have to find a handsome officer to dance with. I refuse to dance with Rockwell."

"Oh, Izzy, maybe you shouldn't provoke him any – "

Izzy waved away Lillian's concern. "He won't even notice. He always makes sure to fill his table with toadies. Including 'young and bouncy' women eager for his attention – and his money. Oh!" Izzy said, suddenly remembering. She searched for a letter among her papers and handed it to Lillian. "This came in the morning's mail. Addressed to you."

Lillian raised her face in surprise. "Mail for me?" She took the letter and read the return address. "Mrs. Huntington, Artistic Director. I don't know her. It must have to do with Artists for Victory. Probably asking for more involvement. I'll have to see what I can do." She set the letter aside.

"I don't see how that's possible. You're already volunteering two nights a week and most weekends."

"I love teaching the patients," Lillian said. "It's always new and fresh, and so gratifying. But with Charles's leave coming up, I can't take on anything more. Perhaps in the new year I can add another evening."

"Do you have a date for his arrival?"

Lillian sat up. "No, but it could be any day. He'll have to spend a week at headquarters in Virginia, but then he'll be home for three weeks. Three weeks, Izzy! We'll have Christmas together and we're going to celebrate our anniversary early – our third! Can you believe it?"

Linda Mahkovec

"Seems impossible," Izzy said, shaking her head at the passage of time. "So, he'll be here in time for the school Christmas show? Tommy and Gabriel must be beside themselves with joy."

"They are. They've been working hard on ideas for their play." Lillian lowered her voice and glanced to her side. "I almost feel guilty. It will be a sad Christmas for so many people."

Izzy nodded and considered her words. Then she straightened, and took a deep breath. "This war can't last forever." She gave her friend a parting smile.

Lillian took the letter and tucked it into her purse. Another mysterious letter. She mused on the back-to-back letters she had recently received from Ursula, the elder daughter of Charles's sister, Kate. First Ursula had written about the farm, news of her brothers, a few of the wartime recipes they were trying out, and how Jessica was busy with student teaching, having decided on becoming a grade school teacher.

She also wrote about the Christmas present she and Jessica were making for Kate – a quilt, with a piece of embroidery in the center depicting the farm – "based on the drawing you made, Aunt Lillian." Lillian clearly remembered the sketch she had made when she and Charles and the boys visited in '41 – the summer before the war. Then the letter closed with Ursula asking if she could perhaps visit Lillian in the spring for a few weeks.

Lillian had thought it a wonderful idea, but before she could answer the letter, she received the crushing news from Kate saying that her eldest son, Eugene, had been shot down somewhere over France or Belgium, and that, as yet, there was no word, either of his death or capture. A second letter from Ursula soon followed saying that she would not be visiting after all, and not to mention the letter to her mother. Puzzling.

Kate had already lost one son, Francis; Lillian prayed that she wouldn't lose another. Kate's letter said that until they heard otherwise, they were going to assume Eugene was alive. She wrote that her daughters were her mainstay and that she was grateful for their energy and optimism. And though it must have been difficult for Kate to do, she also mentioned her gratitude for the three POWs who worked on the farm.

What a time. Kate praising prisoners of the same army that killed one son and shot down another. She tried to imagine three Germans working on Kate's farm – and couldn't. And yet she knew Kate counted herself lucky to have the same POWs for a year now.

Lillian knew that Ursula would stand by her mother and do whatever was necessary to get through these difficult times. But why had she wanted to come to New York City? Lillian imagined that the beautiful young girl, eighteen now, was bored on the Illinois farm and wanted to get away – the exact way she had felt at that age.

Lillian thought of the charm and effervescence of youth, and picked up her pencil. She added a hint of a dimple on the pretty girl reaching for the bar of soap, and smiled at the result.

*

Lillian and her younger son, ten-year-old Gabriel, left the hospital drawing class and caught the bus home. For a while, she had stopped bringing Tommy and Gabriel to the Artists for Victory classes, where they had sometimes assisted, passing out supplies to the veterans and helping her to clean up. There were so many gravely injured men, and the psychological wounds were increasing as the war raged on. Though the boys had seen their share of the wounded in the wards over the past year, Lillian had made the decision to keep them away from the classroom. Instead, Gabriel now helped out in the recreation room, where soldiers who would soon be discharged spent much of their time. Tommy, thirteen years old, was increasingly busy with Boy Scouts and school projects.

On their way home, they stopped to pick up Tommy, who was with his friends, Mickey and Amy. The eighth-graders were working on a short play for the school Christmas program.

Tommy was soon pulling on his coat and recapping their progress. Lillian smiled to hear that Amy, a confident girl that Tommy was sweet on, was going to be the director. Gabriel gave a cheer of delight to hear that his friend Billy, Mickey's younger brother, would also have a bit part in the play.

Tommy abandoned all talk of the play when he realized how hungry he was. "I'm starving, Mom," he said. "What's for dinner?"

Lillian was too tired to think about it. "How about we go to the diner tonight?"

Tommy and Gabriel raised their heads in surprise.

"You mean it?" asked Tommy.

"I'd say we all deserve it. Gabriel spent the last two hours assisting the volunteers in the recreation room while I taught my classes, and you've been working all evening on your play."

"Can I have a chocolate sundae?" asked Gabriel.

Lillian laughed at his question. "Let's think about dinner first. Then we'll see about dessert."

They settled into a booth, looked over the menu, and placed their orders.

"Don't forget, Mom," said Gabriel, "tomorrow's Tuesday. We need money for stamps at school. This time it's for the 'Buy a Jeep' campaign."

"And I need to pay for a model plane kit for Scouts."

"All right," said Lillian, making a mental note. She listened with interest to all the updates on what happened at school, and soon their meals arrived.

"So, tell me more about the drama," said Lillian. "You have your main players – what about the plot? Have you made a decision?"

"We're sticking with the idea of the soldier from the Great War who makes it home in time for Christmas," said Tommy.

"It was my idea," said Gabriel, "and I still don't have a role."

"We'll think of something. But it's a really short play, Gabe. We can't go over thirty minutes."

"They don't like the other part of my idea," he said, turning to Lillian. "I said I could be a fox who helps the soldier cross over no-man's-land and through enemy lines, and then – "

"Gabriel, there are no foxes in foxholes," Tommy explained yet again.

"But maybe there was in *his* foxhole."

Tommy rolled his eyes to the ceiling, and bit into his sandwich.

"What did you and the volunteers do tonight, Gabriel?" Lillian asked, changing the subject.

Gabriel rubbed his chin and scrunched up his mouth, as if searching for an answer from the deep past. "Well, if I recollect correctly – "

"Oh, no," groaned Tommy, "more Henry talk."

"Is that what Henry says?" Lillian asked, amused.

"Only when he's trying to remember something," explained Gabriel. He smiled at the sundae that was just being placed in front of him. "Tonight, I helped out with ping pong. Henry was the referee and I chased down the balls. Mrs. Coppel is setting up a tournament for Christmas. Everyone puts in a quarter and the champion gets all the money." Gabriel tilted his bowl and scooped up some ice cream. "Sometimes Henry takes a jar and stands outside the hospital and asks for money. If it's not too cold. Sometimes he puts in his own money. I put in a nickel tonight."

"You'll have to introduce me to Henry. I know many of the volunteers, but not the new ones."

"He knows you."

"Does he? Perhaps I've met him. You say he's a veteran?"

Gabriel nodded and scraped out the last of the ice cream.

"Well, you can introduce me to him next time. Finish up, boys. It's getting late."

Lillian glanced at the bill and reached for her purse. When she took out her wallet she saw the letter. "I forgot all about this." She opened it and began to read, puzzling over the contents. Then her eyes widened and she let out a gasp.

"What? What, Mom?" Tommy asked, nervously cracking his knuckles.

"Dad's still coming home, isn't he?" asked Gabriel.

Lillian's smile widened and she set the letter down. "I can't believe it!"

"What?" Tommy asked, growing impatient. "Tell us!"

"Yeah, tell us, Mom."

"It's good news." She glanced at the letter again, and shook her head in disbelief. "It's from a woman I met two years ago, when I took my portfolio around, looking for work as an illustrator."

"When you wanted to quit the switchboard?" asked Tommy.

"Yes. I showed my drawings to this woman and she wants to meet with me. After two years!"

"What took her so long?" asked Tommy.

"Well, now she's the head of the department. Imagine that! She writes that she wanted to get in touch with me months ago, but didn't know how to reach me. I was supposed to follow up with her, but …" Lillian looked out at the floor, trying to remember what had prevented her. "I just got so busy with everything, I guess. Anyway, she says she passed by Rockwell Publishing the other day, and suddenly remembered my saying that I worked there."

"Are you going to work for her now?" asked Gabriel.

Lillian folded the letter and slipped it back into her purse. "Oh, I don't know what will come of it. But she wants me to stop by and bring my portfolio." Lillian tried to push down her enthusiasm. "It probably doesn't mean anything, but it's nice to know that she remembered me." She took a sip of coffee and paid the bill, still smiling.

*

That night after the boys were in bed, Lillian sat up late assessing her portfolio, wishing that she had more drawings to show to Mrs. Huntington that were not war-related. But there just hadn't been the time. When she wasn't at work, she was at the hospital, or busy with the boys. Much of her time at home was spent knitting for Bundles for Bluejackets, or sewing for the Red Cross, and…

Lillian realized she was just making excuses. The truth was she had set her dreams aside. But now here was a woman – an art director! – who wanted to see her drawings – in particular, those of women and children. A surge of excitement shot through her, and her old dreams burst into life.

She glanced over at the framed photographs on the bookshelves, and let her eyes rest on the picture she took of Charles three years ago, soon after their marriage. She could hardly wait to see him. For the first time in years, things were looking up. Charles would be home soon, and she would have this good news to share.

She leaned back, remembering his visit in the spring. Just before he left they had argued, and she had regretted it ever since. She made sure that every letter she had since written was full of cheer, and that she knew what a lucky woman she was to have him and the boys – and that nothing else mattered. All she wanted was the war to be over, and his safe return.

Soon she would be able to show him that she meant it. She put her portfolio away, filled with the heady sense of second chances.

*

Under a dark mottled sky at end of day, a crowded Liberty ship cut through the waters of the Atlantic, on a zigzag course homebound. Charles Drooms leaned against the railing, his happiness increasing with each hour, each minute that brought him closer to Lillian.

From long practice, he scanned the horizon and sky for signs of the enemy, though his thoughts were with the one person who meant everything in the world to him. In his hands were well-worn photographs of Lillian and the boys, barely visible in the fading light.

He looked down at the family photo and thought of Tommy and Gabriel, thirteen and ten now – hard to believe. They were just little boys when he first met them four years ago. He smiled down at the photograph. He had missed out on nearly a whole year of their lives. They tugged at his heart in a way that surprised him. The strength of it. It couldn't have been stronger had he been their real father, their blood father.

He slid the family picture behind his favorite photo – a close-up of Lillian, eyes on the camera, eyes on him. And a deeper tug pulled at him. Part love, part sorrow. My God, he thought, how he missed her and longed to hold her again.

He tried not to think about the distance that had come between them on his last visit. The orders for him to fly back to Europe had come sooner than expected and they hadn't had time to patch things up. He was left with a sense of remorse at having squandered precious time over things that didn't matter. A senseless string of disagreements that he couldn't even remember very well.

It started when he had inadvertently let it slip about his illness in the previous fall, and she was furious that he had kept it from her. And she was becoming worried they would not have children together. The war was making sure of that; they had so little time together. He tried to ignore the words she had said about his age having something to do with it. Rather than point out that it was just as likely to be her age that was an issue, he had kept silent. But then she had become angry at his silence, and one thing led to another. He remembered the two nights they had slept on separate sides of the bed – the first time ever. And then, just when he decided to address the issue, the call had come. And he had to leave.

Though they had tried to repair the rift with letters full of love and assurance, the thought had haunted him ever since. Had he taken something away from Lillian, in his own selfishness to have her? Would she have been happier with a younger man? Their age difference of ten years had never been an issue before, but now he questioned it.

He shifted his focus to this trip, and how he would make everything right. A week in Virginia for meetings and debriefing, and then home. Home. Christmas with the boys – a tree, their school play, perhaps a trip to Lillian's sister upstate. And an early anniversary celebration. He smiled as he thought of the gift for her that he had found in an antique shop in London – a Victorian sapphire ring, set with tiny diamonds and seed pearls. It suited her perfectly.

He let out a deep sigh that was more like a moan. Yes, a month at home. But then, in all likelihood, he would head out to the West Coast, and on to the Pacific where they would, at continued

great cost, conclude the war with Japan. The war in
Europe was at last coming to an end. It had been
a long, strife-filled year. In addition to fighting a
relentless enemy, there had been the unexpected
setbacks – mud and rain, the almost impassable
ditches and dense hedgerows in Normandy, and
now, terrible cold weather was setting in. But the
end with Germany was in sight, and they could
focus all efforts on Japan. Many more bitter years lay
ahead. Like everyone, he was worn out, exhausted
by the toll of war, disgusted at the degradation of
humanity.

Charles put a halt to those thoughts and
gazed again at the photographs. If he had to head
to the Pacific, he hoped he could take a train out
west, and stop by to see his sister, Kate. It would be
good to spend some time in the country, far away
from the destructive horrors of war. He even enter-
tained the idea of perhaps bringing Lillian and the
boys with him.

He held the picture of Lillian closer to his
eyes, and his lips softened in a smile. He had to
put the photo away, or that expression of love in
her eyes would begin to overwhelm him. One last
look –

He became aware of footsteps approaching,
and soon Corporal Willie Gannon was leaning
against the railing next to him.

"Evening, Willie."

Willie pointed his chin to the horizon.
"Staring out towards home isn't going to make it
come any faster." He looked down at the image of

Lillian. "Well, I'd be staring too, if I had that to go home to."

Charles smiled. He was grateful that Willie wasn't the type of soldier to add a comment like, "hope she hasn't found someone else to warm her bed," or one of the other comments that were bandied about. Couldn't blame the men – so many of them had received Dear John letters.

Willie shook out a cigarette from his pack. "Smoke?" He always stood to the right of people, when possible. The right side of his face was puckered and twisted with scars from two years ago – El Alamein.

Charles declined the offer, but took the pack of matches from Willie and struck the match for him – a routine they had established since leaving port.

Charles slid the photos inside his jacket, placing a protective hand over them as was his habit. "Another few days, and we'll be able to see the coastline."

"We would have seen it by now if it weren't for the damned U-boats – all this zig-zagging our way across the Atlantic. And yet we know they're out there." He, too, scanned the waters as he spoke. Then shook his head. "Bringing back a ship full of POWs. I can't help thinking we got it all backwards. It should be full of our own men."

"A few more months," said Charles. "The war in Europe will soon be over, and then the ships *will* be full of our own men."

Willie gave a sarcastic laugh. "Right. On their way to the Pacific."

Charles didn't want to think about the years ahead. "Have you noticed? The POWs are getting younger and younger – and older. Young boys and old men. They look too dispirited to put up much of a fight."

Willie took a long, slow draw on his cigarette, and blew the smoke out the side of his mouth. "Oh, there's some dangerous ones among them. You can feel it in the way they look at you – they'd love nothing more than to put a knife in your gut. But yeah, the younger ones." He shook his head again. "You can hear them at night crying for their mothers. '*Mutti, Mutti.*' Kids, some of them. Breaks your heart. And most of them have nothing to go back home to when it's finally all over. Just a bunch of rubble. But serves the bastards right. They all should have stood up to Hitler years ago. And none of this would've happened."

They ignored the fact that when trouble started with Hitler, some of these prisoners were small children.

A deep cough overtook Charles for a moment.

"Good thing you don't smoke," Willie said. He studied Charles for a moment. "You okay? You look beat."

"Fine, fine. Nothing a good night's sleep won't fix."

Willie took a few more pulls on his cigarette, and then flicked it into the churning waters below. "Well, don't stay out too late, old man. You'll miss chow."

Charles smiled at Willie as he left, avoiding looking at the missing arm that was sending the young man home.

Chapter 2

Ursula heard the Ford pickup pulling up to the farmhouse. She went to the window and watched her mother, sister, and her sister's friend make their way to the porch, their arms full of groceries and supplies from town. She hurried to the chair next to the phone in the hallway, and picked up the receiver.

When they came in the front door, they found her chatting in girlish conversation, her legs stretched out in front of her.

"I'd love to, Dolores. I wouldn't miss it for the world. Is there anything I can bring?"

Jessica raised her eyebrows, and Ursula pulled in her legs so they wouldn't have to step over her on their way into the kitchen.

"That'll be swell. I'll be on the 10:45." A burst of laughter. "Me too. See you on Saturday, then."

Kate glanced at her elder daughter, who, after hanging up the phone, came into the kitchen to help put the groceries away.

"Ursula, don't tell me you're going to Peoria again? Why, that'll be three times in the last two months!"

"You don't mind, do you, Mom? Dolores is throwing a going-away party for her brother and I told her I'd be there. I'll be back the next day."

"No. I'm just surprised, is all." She placed her hand on Ursula's cheek and smiled at her, secretly relieved that her daughter's state of mind had finally changed. For months Ursula had been distracted, moody, staring out the windows, and quarreling with Jessica. There were more highs and lows – and almost a false gaiety about her at times. Though when no one was looking, Kate saw despair in her face. Eugene, thought Kate, and shifted her thoughts away from her eldest son. Her eyebrows remained pinched. "Though I don't like to see you traveling alone."

Ursula groaned in amusement. "I'm eighteen, Mom. Besides, Dolores meets me at the train station."

"You'll have to bake something to take with you. We have enough sugar for some spice bread or cookies."

"I offered, but she said there was no need." Ursula opened the oven to check on the cutlets in gravy she had prepared. "Dinner's almost ready," she said.

"Nonsense," said Kate. "You can't arrive to a host's house empty handed." She reached for a basket in the pantry. "I'll put some calico in here and we'll fill it with cookies."

"What an adventure!" cried Shirley, Jessica's best friend. She and Jessica sat at the table, resuming their work on a large canvas banner for the Christmas dance in a few weeks.

Jessica had followed the exchange with curiosity. "Since when are you and Dolores such good friends?"

Ursula tucked her chin in surprise. "Since our plans to go to college. Don't forget we were going to be roommates. Before the war."

"Hmm. It's just not like you to go gallivanting around like that."

Ursula took the flour bag, cut it open, and began to fill up the canister. "Gallivanting? Hardly. I'm going to Peoria. I – I just feel like living a little. It gets tiresome here on the farm. Same routine, day in, day out."

Jessica leaned her head to one side, eyeing her sister.

"Besides," Ursula said with a sly smile, "Dolores knows some swell boys. Men. Some of them are officers."

Shirley sat up, eager for details.

"Aha!" said Kate. "Now it makes more sense." She suddenly brightened. "I have an idea. Why don't you take the girls with you? They could stay with Cousin Violet. She'd be more than happy to pick them up from the party and have them for the night. She could even pick you up from Dolores's the next day and take you all to the train station."

Shirley gasped in hopeful surprise.

Kate smiled. "I'm sure they'd enjoy seeing something new and meeting new people. I know farm life can be a little lonely at times."

Ursula placed the lid on the canister and brushed the flour from her hands. Then she turned around and smiled. "That sounds wonderful. Dolores will be pleased. And I could use the company. The train ride gets monotonous after a while."

"Oh, what fun!" cried Shirley, clasping her hands. "Wait'll I tell Sue Ellen."

Jessica put her hand on her hip. "Shirley Bloomfield, what are you thinking? We promised to help with the Red Cross Christmas parcels. They're counting on us! And I'm in charge of the junior high school students. We can't back out now."

"Oh." Shirley plopped back in her chair. "Right," she said with a sigh.

"What's going in the packages this year?" asked Ursula, changing the subject. She took some canned goods and set them in the pantry just off the kitchen.

"Candy, sunglasses, uniform buttons, playing cards," said Shirley, without much energy. "Same as last year."

"And books and V-mail stationary," said Jessica, with more enthusiasm. "And handkerchiefs – khaki for soldiers, white for sailors."

Ursula shrugged. "Well, that's far more important than a party. Don't worry. There will be others."

Shirley sagged in disappointment, and continued drawing the letters on the banner to spell *Merry Christmas to Our Men in Uniform*!

Kate left to park the truck by the machine shed.

As soon as the back door closed behind her, Jessica addressed her sister. "You don't fool me, Ursula. You knew we wouldn't be able to go. What are you and Dolores up to?"

"For goodness' sake, Jessica. It's just a simple party. We're not *up to* anything." She opened the cupboard and began taking out the plates.

"I'll bet she has a beau," whispered Shirley, her eyes bright.

Jessica frowned at the idea, never taking her eyes off her sister. "Why is it so last minute?" she asked.

"Why do you think? Her brother was called up. It's her youngest brother. And they're sad to see him go." Ursula set the plates at the opposite end of the table. "So, they're throwing a going-away party for him."

"What a shame, though," said Shirley. "Our POWs are finally back from working on the levee, and I wouldn't have been missed. I could easily have gone this weekend." She traced another letter and sighed at the lost opportunity. "Have yours returned?" she asked Jessica. "I haven't seen them in a while. Funny how you miss them when they're gone."

"Gustav and Karl are back," said Jessica, "but Friedrich's still over at the river. Ever since they found out he speaks English, they use him as a go-between. If we knew he was going to be gone for so long, we never would have let him go. Would we, Ursula?"

The color rose to Ursula's cheeks. "Listen to you. You talk as if we own them."

"I didn't mean that," protested Jessica. "I just meant that we have more chores to do when they're not here. And Friedrich's been gone for over a month now. A month and a half. I would have thought you missed him, too."

Ursula's head snapped up and she nailed Jessica with a piercing glance.

Jessica avoided her stare and smoothed out the banner. "Poor Ursula has had to do most of the milking. Gustav usually does it, but with Friedrich gone, he's needed out in the fields and on repairs." She took a step back and studied Shirley's work. "Since when are there two *T*s in Christmas?"

"Oh, no!" groaned Shirley. She reached for the eraser and began to rub out her mistake.

Ursula checked on the noodles, and finding them tender, drained the water. The lid slipped and the noodles splashed into the sink. "Now look what you've made me do!"

"Me? It's not my fault you're so clumsy," said Jessica. Then under her breath she added, "Seems like everyone's mind is on something else."

Kate overheard the bickering when she came back in. "Now what?"

Ursula looked over her shoulder and smiled. "Jessica says I'm clumsy. And she's right. Look. I just dumped all the noodles." She began scooping them up, and rinsing them.

"Is that all?" asked Kate, relieved. "Are you staying for dinner, Shirley?"

"I'd love to, but I'm going to catch a ride home with Ed. I promised Sue Ellen to help with dinner. Joe's coming by and she'll be in a tizzy making sure that everything is just right."

"My, my," said Jessica. "What people do for love."

*

On Saturday, Kate took out the old Studebaker sedan to take Ursula to the train station. They stopped at the Bloomfield's to pick up Shirley, her older sister Sue Ellen, and their mother to do their weekly shopping. Jessica and Shirley would spend all day at the American Legion Hall, putting together the GI Christmas packages, and catch a ride back home in the evening with Mr. Bloomfield.

Ursula had taken special care with her appearance, wearing her good dove-gray coat and hat, and a purple scarf tucked about her neck that matched her amethyst earrings. She wore her one pair of dress shoes, her kid leather gloves, and had even put on a little lipstick, something she rarely did. She had let her hair grow long over the past year, and it now hung in soft dark waves down her back. Several people looked on admiringly: Ursula was a vision of loveliness. She was in apparent high spirits as the train sounded its approach in the distance.

Kate tried not to stare at her daughter, and yet she couldn't help herself. The past year had deepened Ursula's beauty. Her contrariness remained, but it was tempered with a softness.

There was a new maturity about her, thought Kate. More woman-like, which was to be expected with the war and all; she was called upon to be an adult. But it made Kate sad to think that Ursula's girl-hood was already behind her.

As she gazed on her daughter, the worri-some notion that had been bothering her of late prodded her afresh – as if there was something on the periphery of knowing. But Kate had learned to brush away such worries. Whenever she looked at Ursula, she was immediately reminded of Eugene. They both had those startling deep blue eyes, the dark wavy hair, and a vulnerability behind the outer strength that made her want to protect them. As was her habit now, Kate marshalled her thoughts to imagine Eugene in uniform, strong and capable, unhurt. They would have word soon.

Kate again noticed the unusual gaiety about Ursula. It was good to see her out of her overalls and work shoes for a change. "You look lovely, Ursula. I'm happy you're getting out a bit. Having a lit-tle fun." Everything was fine. Ursula was fine. And Eugene was fine. Kate lifted her chin and smiled at the people from town. Patiently answered their sympathetic looks and questions about Eugene.

"No word yet, but we'll hear from him soon."

A cloud of sadness briefly darkened Ursula's face, and she squeezed her mother's hand.

Mrs. Bloomfield and Sue Ellen were mak-ing a fuss over Ursula.

"Just look at you!" said Sue Ellen. "Traveling all by yourself, dressing all fancy. Going to parties and meeting new people."

"You'll break the hearts of the boys, if you're not careful, my dear," added Mrs. Bloomfield with an indulgent smile.

Ursula threw her head back and laughed away the comment.

Sue Ellen leaned in to Ursula and whispered. "Tell me the truth, do you have a beau?"

Ursula whispered back. "Maybe I do. But don't say a word."

Sue Ellen giggled and zipped her lips.

The station grew more crowded and goodbyes became more urgent to the men in uniform. Happier people lined the platform, smiling in anticipation at the arrival of their sons, brothers, and husbands. The whistle blew, and the train could be seen following the curved tracks into town. Several servicemen waved from the windows, while others stood in the open door, scanning the awaiting crowd as the train slowed and came to a stop.

The GIs were the first to climb down the stairs from the train, followed by the other passengers. Embraces and tears, laughter and smiles filled the crowd, and people were jostled by duffle bags, suitcases, and elbows as they made their way to and away from the train.

Ed, Kate's old farmhand, had driven into town for supplies, and now parked his old red pickup truck close to the station to observe the spectacle.

"Why, there's Kate and the girls," he said to Otto, the guard for the three POWs who worked on the farm. Ed opened the creaky truck door. "Let's go say hello. See Ursula off."

"Come on, boys," Otto said, motioning to the POWs seated in the back of the truck.

Though the German prisoners and the townspeople had gotten used to each other over the past year, the POWs maintained a quiet demeanor in town. Except for the youngest, Karl, who perked up at any gathering and grinned from ear to ear at all the commotion.

Ed, followed by Otto and the POWs, snaked his way through the crowd towards Kate and Ursula.

Kate brushed at her daughter's coat. "Make sure you keep an eye on your belongings. And be sure to invite Dolores here. It's always polite to reciprocate. And make sure the cookies don't get crushed. And be careful."

Ursula took her overnight bag from her mother and kissed her cheek. "Mom, I'll be back tomorrow."

Kate had to smile. "All right, all right. I'll be here to pick you up. Have yourself a good time." She walked with Ursula to the train.

Shirley pulled her sister's arm and said excitedly, "I'll bet you anything she has a boyfriend. Maybe even a fiancé. An officer!"

Sue Ellen primped a bit, feeling that some of Ursula's glamour had rubbed off on her. "I'm not saying she does or she doesn't." She gave what she hoped was a knowing smile. "But *if* she does, it would be just like her, a city boy being much closer to her tastes. She never has liked the boys round here."

"You should be the last person to complain about that," Shirley said.

"Joe was over her a long time ago," protested Sue Ellen. "He told me so."

"If you say so," said Shirley.

"Look!" cried Jessica. "Here's Ed." She greeted the group of men who had just stepped up. "And Friedrich is back," she added, her eyes on Ursula.

Ursula gave a start and her smile dropped. Friedrich was not expected until next week. How long had he been watching? How much had he heard?

Kate spun around at the news. "Welcome Friedrich! We're glad to have you back."

Friedrich nodded his thanks.

"Mornin', Kate," said Ed, and put his finger to his hat in greeting to the others. He then smiled at his favorite. "Mornin', Ursula. We saw you as we pulled in. Thought we'd come and see you off."

"Hello, Ed. Otto." Ursula nodded to the three POWs who hung back.

"Ursula is off to Peoria – again," Jessica explained.

Friedrich's eyes shot to Ursula. She lowered her gaze and tugged at her gloves.

"Well, look at you!" said Otto. "You're becoming quite the traveler. And all dressed up. Must have a gentleman friend somewhere," he said with a grin.

"What takes you this time, Ursula?" Ed asked over Otto's comment.

Before she could answer, Sue Ellen blurted, "Parties and dancing with handsome officers!"

"Going to Peoria to break some hearts," Mrs. Bloomfield added.

Ursula swallowed and ignored the comments. "I'm just going to see my friend Dolores. I'll be back tomorrow, Ed." She cast a quick glance at Friedrich, before climbing the stairs to the train.

Jessica held up the basket of cookies. "Don't forget this – for the party."

Ursula tapped her head at her forgetfulness. "Oh, of course."

As Ursula reached for the basket, Jessica held onto it for a brief moment, forcing Ursula to look at her.

"Have a good time! Say hello to Dolores."

Ursula smiled goodbye, cringing at the comments that trailed behind her.

"I'll bet you anything she has a beau," said Shirley again.

Mrs. Bloomfield sighed. "No one looks that lovely unless they're in love."

Ursula flashed around, almost begging them all to stop.

But they simply smiled and waved goodbye. Sue Ellen winked at her old friend and zipped her lips again.

Ursula entered the train and soon found a seat by the window. She set the basket on the seat next to her, and waved goodbye. Friedrich's stoic gaze met hers and pierced her to the core.

The whistle sounded and the train began to chug through the town, picking up speed as it headed out into the country.

Ursula handed her ticket to the porter. She was grateful that the seat next to her remained empty and that lively conversation filled the row behind her. She turned her face to the window, and reached into her purse for a handkerchief. Then she held it to her eyes, to catch her falling tears.

Christmastime 1944

Chapter 3

Lillian glanced at the clock. Tommy and Gabriel would be home soon and she needed to get started on dinner. She made a final stitch, tied a knot and bit off the thread, and then set aside her sewing. After reading Ursula's letter about the quilt that she and Jessica were making for Kate, she felt inspired to do something with the remnants she had been saving: old dresses, a floral apron, and extra fabric from the calico curtains she had made. Though there wasn't enough to make a large quilt, she had started on the project. It was a nice change from the knitting she still did regularly for the Red Cross and Bundles for Blue Jackets.

She was soon lifting the lid on the pasta, inhaling the scent of butter, onions, mushrooms, and thyme. She wanted to try out a new recipe before making it for Charles. The rationing taught her how to cook without the reliance on meat, and she was surprised at how simple it was to make a meal without any meat at all. She had carefully rationed her coupons and had several meals planned out for when he arrived home.

As she washed tomatoes and cucumbers for a small salad, she determined that nothing would get in the way of Charles having a relaxing, happy time at home. Their time together in the spring, for the most part, had been absolute paradise. A shiver ran through her as she remembered their time together. How she had met him at the train station, the moment when her eyes first found him in the crowd. She had known that he had moved from the North Atlantic to the Mediterranean – but was not prepared for how tanned he was. He was so handsome, she thought with a shy smile. He melted her every single time she beheld him, and she knew that would never change. But then her smile slowly disappeared as she remembered the distance that had come between them right before he left.

She placed the tomatoes and cucumbers on the cutting board, and began slicing them. If only they could have had another few days to patch over things. It wasn't that *she* felt she had to have another child. But she had so wanted it for Charles. She stopped and stared out at nothing. It wasn't for lack of trying, she thought, her face softening – then she began slicing another cucumber. But perhaps she had worried too much about it, as Charles had suggested. Her anxiety that she might not conceive had made her touchy and overly sensitive. Words were exchanged, feelings were stepped on, and she had let it come between them.

After he left, she had watched for signs of pregnancy. Then two weeks later, her anxiety had grown into excitement at what she believed was morning sickness. But it had turned out to be the flu. She had become convinced that there would be no more children. And she was at peace with it. Like Charles said, they had Tommy and Gabriel, they had each other – what more could they possibly want?

She slid the cucumbers and tomatoes into a bowl, and added a little vinegar and oil. Well, this time would be different. No arguments. Just love and happiness. She ground salt and pepper over the salad, lightly tossed it, and set it on the table.

She smiled as she heard the boys running up the stairs, and the door soon burst open.

"I can smell that in the hallway!" said Tommy. "What is it? I'm starved!"

"Freshly made gnocchi from Mancetti's. With onions and mushrooms." She lifted the lid for them to look inside.

"And garlic bread?" asked Gabriel, sniffing the air.

Lillian nodded. "Go wash up. It's almost ready."

In a few minutes, Tommy took his seat at the table.

"Good news, Mom. We have the whole play worked out," he said, using his hands to set the stage. "The setting is Flanders. The soldier is wounded in the arm and he's been separated from his battalion, and the only way to safety is through enemy lines." He dropped his voice, as if careful not to be overheard. "He has vital information that he must take back to London. After a lot of narrow escapes, he makes it through, catches a ride on a fishing boat and hooks up with his ship. Everyone thought he was dead and they're happy to see him. And he makes it home just in time for Christmas. What do you think?"

"I love it! That's a wonderful story." Lillian placed the bowl of fragrant pasta in the middle of the table and briefly imagined Charles sitting across from her, enjoying the meal. Her face glowed with pleasure.

"What are you smiling at, Mom?" asked Gabriel, sitting down.

"Oh – Tommy was just telling me the plot of the play."

"He has all kinds of close calls," continued Tommy, "and he almost gets caught. But he's really smart and always outwits the enemy." He turned to Gabriel, and added, "On his own."

"They don't like my idea of the helpful fox. Even though Henry said there *could* have been a fox in a foxhole."

"We already made the decision," said Tommy. "No foxes."

They ate in silence for a few moments. Gabriel tapped his fork against his plate as he stared off, squinting at some vision. Then he sat up, smiling.

"How about a ghost?" he asked. "The ghost of his best friend appears in the fog, and – "

"This is a play about Christmas, Gabriel, not Halloween." Tommy leaned forward and took another slice of garlic bread.

"What about Jacob Marlow in *A Christmas Carol*? Rattling his chains."

"The play can only be thirty minutes and it's already too long," said Tommy. "We have to shorten some parts as it is." He took another helping of gnocchi. "By the way, Mom, Gabriel said you would help with the sets and costumes."

Lillian opened her mouth, ready to scold Gabriel. But the sweet look of pride on his face prevented her. "You should have checked with me first."

"All I said was that my mom was an artist and likes to volunteer. Then Miss Dillon said maybe you could make a few drawings and I said, sure."

"You should have asked first, Gabriel. What if I had plans? And once your father comes home all my time is going to be spent with him."

"By then the work will all be done. Besides, you said the busier you are, the more you get done."

"That doesn't mean I want to take on anything more."

"Sorry, Mom. Should I tell her you can't?"

"No. I'll meet with her and see what she has in mind." Though she tried to sound angry, she knew that she could easily take on another project. The truth was, she had become agile at taking on multiple tasks. She could easily take on another ten and manage just fine. The war had taught her how to manage more, on less. She was accomplishing more, in spite of there being less time, fewer resources, rationing –

"Dad will be here for the play, won't he, Mom?" asked Gabriel.

"He'll be here, all right," answered Tommy. "He told me so in his last letter."

Lillian knew from the past several years that delays and the unexpected were always a possibility. She had learned not to believe in firm dates. "If it's in his control, he'll be here in time. He's so looking forward to it."

"We have most of it worked out," said Tommy. "We're still working on parts for Gabriel and Billy."

"Billy said he wants to be the fisherman who finds him on the shore. So what part will I have?"

"We'll figure it out at our next meeting." Tommy got up and poured himself another glass of milk. "And we have to do our research and interviews. That's part of the assignment."

Gabriel held up his glass for Tommy to fill. "How about we ask Mrs. Kuntzman? Her son was in that war."

Tommy turned to Lillian. "Do you think it would make her sad since he was killed at Flanders?"

"I don't know. I think she might like to talk about him. You could ask her."

"And we could ask Henry," added Gabriel. "He was there. He knows all about it."

"Henry, Henry, Henry!" said Tommy. "That's all you talk about anymore. Who is he?"

"I told you. He's a veteran at the hospital."

"Wounded?" challenged Tommy.

"No. He's a volunteer."

"Why isn't he fighting?"

"I guess he's too old," said Gabriel, biting into another piece of garlic bread. "He was in the Great War."

"So was Dad. He's almost fifty but that doesn't stop him."

"Henry said he tried to sign up but they wouldn't take him. Because he was too old."

"Does he have gray hair?" asked Tommy.

Gabriel shook his head. "No."

"Then he's not too old," insisted Tommy. He took another helping of gnocchi.

"He doesn't have any hair. Only a little bit around the edges. And it's white. But he said he lost his hair a long time ago. That most of it was already gone when he rode with Teddy."

Tommy gasped and choked on his milk. "Teddy Roosevelt? He must be ancient!"

"I promised him he could see the play. Can he sit with you and Dad so he has someone to talk to?"

"Of course he can sit with us. And Izzy and Mrs. Kuntzman will be there. Mrs. Wilson is sorry to miss it but she'll be away for Christmas. Still, there will be plenty of people for Henry to talk to. I'll stop by and introduce myself to him the next time I'm at the hospital."

*

Lillian straightened up her desk, slipped on her coat and hat, and left work. As she rode the elevator down to the lobby, she considered how best to celebrate their anniversary – though it would be two months early, she was thrilled at the idea. She briefly considered a night at the Plaza Hotel. She had always dreamed of staying there, of having a room overlooking Central Park. But that was far too extravagant. Besides, she had already come up with several options. Her plan was to gauge Charles's mood and then make a decision. Would he be happy that there was an end in sight to the war in Europe? Or was he worn down by the years of fighting? He might not want to go out for dinner and dancing, in which case she would cook a nice meal at home, and perhaps they could build a fire and sit up late like they used to do.

As she cut through the crowded lobby, she became aware of footsteps clicking nearer. Her arm was suddenly pulled from behind, spinning her around.

"Lilly!"

"My God, Izzy – what is it?" Lillian was always ready for bad news – an attack, a disaster in the war overseas, an explosion at the shipyards – but Izzy was positively beaming. Euphoric.

"I did it!" Her eyes sparkled and her smile became even wider.

"Did what?"

"I quit!"

Lillian's stunned silence caused Izzy to throw her head back in laughter.

"Izzy – you didn't!"

"I did, indeed! I've quit my job. I've left Rockwell Publishing. I've said good riddance to the most unpleasant of men."

"But Izzy – "

"No, no, no! This isn't how you're supposed to respond. Smile! Laugh! Be happy for me!" She looped her arm through Lillian's and pulled her forward. "And don't you *dare* say no to having a celebratory drink with me."

"My God, you're serious."

"I'm serious, all right. Don't look so surprised. I've been threatening it for months. Or has it been years?"

"But I didn't think you really meant it."

"Neither did Rockwell," said Izzy. "I wasn't sure of it myself until I heard the words come tumbling out. Oh, I wish you could have seen his face. Come on. Let me tell you all about it."

They were soon sitting at a window table in a little side street café with a jukebox playing lively music. Several couples, many of the men in uniform, filled the tables.

"Two martinis," Izzy said to the waitress. "Straight up," she added, wriggling out of her coat. She draped it on the seat next to her, folded her hands, and smiled expectantly at Lillian.

Lillian sat across from her, took a deep breath, and shook her head. "I don't know what to say. I have to admit – I'm stunned. You've been there for, what? Over ten years?"

"Yes, and why on earth I stayed for so long is beyond me."

The waitress soon brought their drinks. Izzy lifted her glass to Lillian. "To better times ahead!"

"To better times," said Lillian, raising her glass. She took a small sip, and blinked at the strong drink.

"And to finding a more enjoyable job."

Lillian nodded and took another sip.

"With a more civilized boss," Izzy added.

Lillian pushed her drink aside. "I – I've never really cared for martinis."

Izzy snagged the waitress as she passed by their table. "A glass of sherry for my friend. Or an old-fashioned?" she asked, turning to Lillian.

"Sherry, please."

Izzy reached for Lillian's glass. "Give me that." She downed the rest of her martini, gave her head a quick shake at the effect, and poured Lillian's drink into her glass. She moved her shoulders back and forth to the Andrew Sisters' song playing on the jukebox.

Lillian leaned forward on her elbows. "Tell me again, Izzy – but more slowly. What exactly happened? And are you sure it's final? You won't regret it tomorrow?"

"Absolutely! I'm absolutely sure. One hundred percent." Izzy leaned back in her chair and gazed out the window, looking past the pedestrians and traffic. She tried to remember when this latest argument began. "It all started – or rather, it was a continuation of the argument about rehiring Mr. Casey. You know they never got along. Mr. Casey was always too outspoken. But things are different now. He's desperate for work – he's got two kids and is quite dejected. Battle fatigue, they call it. But besides all that, he's a good worker and Rockwell knows it."

"Yes," Lillian agreed. "I always heard he had that reputation."

Izzy sipped her drink. "The worst of it is that I approached it all wrong. I was too demanding. And I think it cost him the job. I don't think Rockwell really even cares; he just can't back down once he's taken a position. Anyway, I stewed about it all day."

Lillian smiled her thanks as the waitress placed a glass of sherry in front of her. "And then what happened?"

"I took it up again with him and he cut me short. You know what he said?"

Lillian gave a slight shake of her head, waiting.

"He threatened me."

Lillian's eyes grew wide. "Mr. Rockwell threatened you?"

"In his underhanded way. He said, 'You shouldn't be so eager to hire the men back, Miss Briggs. When this war is over, most of you women'll be out of your jobs – if you catch my drift.' He would do it too. It would be just like him to fire me when it's convenient for him to do so."

Lillian held up her glass to the light, admiring the amber translucence before taking a sip. She realized that she would most likely be one of the women to be let go. She tried to determine how she felt about it.

"That really got me thinking. But then I thought – what's wrong with me? This is New York

City. There are jobs everywhere! At five till five I walked into his office." Izzy mimed knocking on his door and pushing it open. "I waited for him to finish his call. I just stood there, smiling sweetly." She demonstrated the smile.

"And?"

"He scowled and leaned forward on his desk. 'I trust you have a good reason for interrupting me. Well, what is it, Miss Briggs?'"

"I calmly stepped up and set the keys on his desk. 'I find that I can no longer work for you. I wish you well. Goodbye, Mr. Rockwell.' And I left. And here I am!" Izzy raised her glass to Lillian and took a sip.

"But – what did he say?"

"He jumped to his feet and got red in the face and waved that obnoxious cigar at me. 'You can't do that!' When I didn't respond, he hollered after me. 'You'll be back! Just like Mr. Casey. They all come back!'"

"And you just left?"

"I just kept on walking." Izzy leaned forward on her elbows, her voice lighter, happier. "Lilly, it felt so good. I can't tell you how liberating it felt." She let out a deep sigh of satisfaction. "I just couldn't take it any longer. And I sure as heck wasn't going to wait for him to fire *me*. I feel like the world has just opened up to me."

"But what will you do? Do you have a plan? Any prospects?"

"Nope! Not a one." Izzy raised her martini again. "Here's to the great unknown!" she said, emptying her glass.

Lillian smiled at Izzy's spirit. She admired her boldness, her decisiveness, and tried to imagine the thrill of a new beginning. "Gosh! I'm happy for you, Izzy."

"There's a worker shortage, after all," she continued. "I know I can find work, and I have money put away. But I don't want to wait. I'm going to start looking tomorrow. I might even try something completely new. Welding."

"Oh, Izzy! You wouldn't do that, would you?"

"Maureen said she could get me a job, like *that*!" Izzy said, snapping her fingers. "This is her second year at the shipyards and she loves it." She cocked her head in consideration. "I think I might be good at it. Or maybe a riveter," she said with a laugh. "Come on. I know you have to be getting home for the boys." She waved for the bill, and reached for her coat.

Lillian took a final sip and pulled on her coat. Suddenly, the jukebox filled the air with Vera Lynn's *I'll be Seeing You*, and Lillian's heart swelled with longing for Charles.

Izzy was at the counter, paying the bill and chatting with the owner, and thought Lillian was right behind her. She walked back in surprise to where Lillian was standing at their table, buttoning up her coat.

"What are you stalling for?"

Lillian gave an embarrassed smile and blinked away her tears. "It's this song. It – Charles says this is the song that most reminds him of us."

Izzy listened to the words and sighed. "I remember when I felt that way about Red." Then she shook away the memory. "Those days are long gone. The lout. He's probably dancing to this song with his wife somewhere in London!" Then she rubbed Lillian's arm. "I'm so happy that Charles will be home soon. You two lovebirds belong together." She took Lillian's arm. "Come on. I need to stop and get a newspaper. I can't wait to see what jobs are available."

The two friends parted ways at the corner. Lillian had to admit that Izzy did seem happier, more carefree. Then it hit her that Izzy wouldn't be at work tomorrow. Or the next day, or the next. And she realized that Izzy was a big reason why she liked her job at Rockwell Publishing. She put her hands in her pockets, thinking that nothing ever stays the same.

*

Charles tossed restlessly in his bunk. Tomorrow. Tomorrow he would be on U.S. soil again. Only a few hours' train ride from Lillian. It was hard to believe. He felt like he was dreaming again. There would be a check-up, a debriefing, a few meetings, some reports to be written – a week at most. And then home. Home for several weeks with Lillian and the boys.

A heavy weariness began to overtake him and he soon fell asleep. But after a few peaceful moments, he woke himself up coughing. Again. He recognized the symptoms, but convinced himself that he was just fatigued.

He sat up and waited for the spasm to pass, and then he propped himself up with his pillow. He needed this visit home – to restore his peace of mind. To remind him that away from all the horror, sweetness and innocence and loveliness still had a place in the world.

It was bad timing that his trip home in the spring was cut short. That long flight back – Newfoundland, Ireland, London. All the while wishing he could do it over again. All he wanted was to see her smile. Then the world would right itself again. How many times had he wished for just an hour with her, just a moment in her embrace.

Another coughing fit overtook him. He stared out into the dimness, remembering the past year. It had been disorienting, the horrors of war mixed with brief respites of wonder – medieval monasteries, ancient cities, the Pyramids. He had stood in awe of humanity's capacity for greatness – and then returned to the nightmare.

He had seen some of the splendors of Europe, and the utter destruction of others. His heart still broke when he thought of Monte Casino. Hundreds of years old, embodying a high ideal, erected to elevate the human spirit. Now a pile of rubble.

He tried to keep his mind fixed on the beautiful and extraordinary things he had seen. Remarkably, from aboard ship at a safe distance, he had witnessed the eruption of Mount Vesuvius. It brought back his younger days when he had studied Roman history. It was as if he had peered through the scrim of time, and caught a glimpse of the eruption that Pliny the Younger had described. His younger days, back when he believed in the intelligence and nobility of mankind. But now?

His estimation of humanity had slipped, then slid, then plummeted as more news came in of the atrocities committed by the Nazis and Japanese. Utter destruction in Europe, devastation in the Pacific, concentration camps, the staggering loss of lives, barbaric cruelty.

He tried to control his thoughts and remember the good. The bravery and sacrifice he had witnessed. But the very juxtaposition of great valor and mass barbarism jarred the mind.

And then there's Japan. He was overcome with a bout of coughing, almost choking him as he tried to catch his breath.

He felt nauseated, hot. Were his thoughts making him sick? He felt his forehead. Another damned fever. He would not succumb. A good night's rest. He must be well. He just needed to sleep. He reached for the photograph of Lillian under his pillow, and though he could barely make out the outline of her face, he felt the darkness leaving him. He took a swig of the cough medicine that contained codeine, and the coughing spasms soon calmed. He slid back down in his pillow and into sweet oblivion, into Lillian's soft arms.

Chapter 4

Ursula made two trips to the chicken coop, hoping to catch sight of Friedrich. She was sick with anguish, desperate to speak to him, to explain away what he had seen at the train station. He hadn't come to the farm on Monday or Tuesday, something he had never done before. In the past year he had never missed a single day. And yesterday, they all worked on the south field fencing and she hadn't seen so much as a glimpse of him.

It had been so long since she had held him, talked with him. Except for the unexpected encounter at the train station, she hadn't seen him since he left to work on the levee. Was he punishing her? Did he doubt her? Is that why he stayed away?

She looked out past the outbuildings, but there was no sign of him. Ed had again taken the POWs to the south field to finish up. Ursula now stood just outside the back porch where her mother and Jessica were doing the laundry. A pall seemed to have settled over the house; the news of Eugene had hit them all hard.

Her attention was caught by the restless flitting and chirping of the tiny sparrows among the branches of the bare lilac bushes. She smiled sadly at the tiny creatures, so small and vulnerable. She held out her hand to them, knowing they were too shy to come near. Still, she wanted to hold them, comfort them, assure them that she would find crumbs to scatter for them in the winter.

The porch door opened. "Ursula?" called Jessica, still wearing her dress from school. "What are you dawdling for? You're supposed to be wringing out the laundry. Come on! It's piling up."

Ursula went inside and helped with the laundry, facing the windows so that she could keep an eye out for Friedrich.

It wasn't until late afternoon, as she was taking the sheets down from the clothesline, that the men returned from the fields. She watched them bring the cart and tools to the machine shed.

Ed touched his hat to her, then addressed Otto. "I'll take Gustav with me to the Martin's to pick up our generator. Back in twenty."

Otto nodded, and he and Karl began to unload the cart in the shed.

Ursula brought the laundry basket into the house, and watched from the window as she loosely folded the clothes. Her heart leapt when she saw Friedrich leave the shed and make his way towards the barn. Jessica and her mother were busy at the kitchen table with the egg and milk accounts and wouldn't notice her absence. She slipped out and entered the barn through the side door.

"Friedrich!"

From across the barn he stopped and looked over at her, and then continued moving the sacks of feed.

Her heart sank. "Friedrich," she said softly, and went to him.

But he kept his attention on the task at hand. "Did you have a good time at the party?"

"I went to see a friend of mine – "

"No lies, Ursula," he said, suddenly facing her. "Just tell me. Do you have someone else? Is that why you go there?"

The blood rushed to her cheeks at his words. She wanted to be angry with him, that he dared to question her love. But she knew he was simply reacting to what he had seen at the train station. And stronger than her anger was her desire to hold him.

"You know me better than that." She walked up to him and embraced him, nestling her head on his chest.

He held her tightly, impulsively. But when she raised her face to him, he avoided her eyes. She placed her hand on his cheek, and turned his face towards hers. "Friedrich. It's been so long since we last saw each other. Aren't you happy to see me?"

"Of course," he said, his voice no more than a whisper. He turned away, cut open a sack of feed, and emptied it into the bin.

"You seem different," Ursula said softly.

"So do you."

Ursula understood the hurt in his eyes, the fear in his voice.

"I'm sorry, Friedrich. I didn't expect you to be there. I didn't expect you until today."

His head snapped up. "Is that how you behave when I am away? You go dancing with the officers? All dressed up. So happy." He set the bag down, and rubbed his face, keeping his back to her. "I'm sorry, Ursula. I'm sorry. I don't blame you." He turned to her. "You are doing what a young girl should be doing. Enjoying your life."

"I know what you're thinking, Friedrich. But it's not like that." She took his hands, and pulled him towards her.

He sank into her embrace and kissed her. Then he buried his head in her hair, her shoulder. "My God, Ursula. You don't know how much I missed you." It almost sounded like a sob and she leaned back to read his face. He started to wrap his arms inside her jacket but she took a step away from him.

He drew back his head, and smiled sadly. "You see? You pull away from me. What is it, Ursula? Do you regret your love for me?"

"Of course not. I – I thought I heard the kitchen door open. Come." She led him to a bale of hay and sat down on it, then examined his face. There were dark shadows under his eyes that were not there before. She caressed his cheek. "You look different, worn. Did they work you too hard? You look thinner, and tired."

He turned his face away.

"Tell me. What was it like? Did you like the river?"

He nodded but kept his eyes down. Then he dropped his elbows on his knees and put his head in his hands.

"What is it? Have you been ill? Not sleeping?"

She waited for him to speak, and placed her hand on his shoulder. "Did something happen at the camp? Friedrich?"

He clenched his eyes shut, as if avoiding a painful vision. She saw that he was pressing his lips together, to stop their trembling.

"My God, what is it, Friedrich?"

"I – When I came back   " He raised his head to speak, but then suddenly jumped up and moved aside. "Someone comes. On the road."

Ursula had been keeping her eyes on the house, and had neglected the other direction. She went to the opening of the barn and peered at the figure coming up the lane. A man in a navy blue peacoat, carrying a duffle bag. She took a few steps forward, and stared harder. Then gasped. Then screamed.

"Jimmy!" she yelled, and ran out of the barn and across the farmyard.

"Jimmy!" She ran down the lane to meet her brother. He set the bag down, and took off his cap, waving it high in the air.

Jessica had heard Ursula's shriek of joy and was now running down the front steps, also calling out to her brother. "Jimmy! Mom, Jimmy's home!"

Ursula reached him first. He caught her and swung her around. "Jimmy! Why didn't you tell us? When – "

Jessica ran up to him, nearly toppling him over, and he swung her around too.

Jessica brushed her tears away and punched him in the arm. "Why didn't you tell us you were coming?" She squeezed him again.

"I wanted to surprise you all. Look at you two! So grown up – in two years! Holy smokes! You're both a head taller since I left."

"You're on leave? Oh, how long can you stay?" asked Ursula, flooded with joy.

Jessica reached for his cap and put it on. Ursula realized she hadn't seen Jessica this playful for a long time. One of their brothers was home! Was safe!

Both sisters talked over each other in their happiness, impatient to have answers to their questions. "How long do you have? Where did you ship into? How did you get home?" In between laughing and hugging him, Jimmy tried to explain as much as he could. He picked up his duffle bag and hoisted it over his shoulder, and, with each sister grabbing an arm, they walked towards the farmhouse.

Then Jimmy suddenly stopped. Kate stood on the porch.

For a moment, they stood silent, their eyes filling with joy.

Then Kate walked down the stairs, then ran – her apron flapping in the December wind. "Jimmy!"

As she approached, both daughters saw that their mother's cheeks were wet with tears, but that she was trying to control her emotions.

"Jimmy!" Kate cried. "Oh, my sweet boy! You're home!" She clung to him tightly, trying her hardest not to cry.

Jimmy dropped his duffle bag, and embraced her, patting her back. "It's okay, Ma. Everything's going to be okay."

She raised her face to his. "You heard about…"

Jimmy nodded as if it were an insignificant detail. "Still no word? Well, don't you worry about Eugene. If I know him, he's probably in some snug farmhouse being fed French food by the farmer's daughter. Just you wait. We'll be getting a letter soon."

Kate smiled at the hopeful vision. "I'm sure you're right. Oh, let me take a look at you!" She leaned back and filled her eyes with her second born, tears welling up in her eyes.

Jimmy squeezed his mother again. "Now, none of that! I told you, everything is going to be A-okay! Come on, let's go inside. You and Jessica without your coats. You must be freezing!"

"How long can you stay, Jimmy?" asked Kate.

Jimmy began to heft his duffle bag over his shoulder again, but Jessica insisted she could carry it. Ursula laughed at her struggle, and taking one handle, they carried it between them.

"I got lucky. I have a month's leave," he said, wrapping his arm around his mother's shoulder. "The ship won't be ready before then."

"A month?" cried Jessica, almost tripping over the bag. "That means you'll be here for Christmas!"

Kate held his arm tightly, and with Jessica alternately asking him questions and then telling him her news, they made their way to the house.

Jessica pointed to Otto, Karl, and Friedrich who were watching from outside the machine shed. "Those are our German workers," she said. "The POWs." She waved at them with her other hand. "It's Jimmy come home!" she called out to them.

Jimmy squinted at them and frowned. "I have a thing or two to say about *that*. Where's Ed? I don't see him out there."

"He's over at the Martin farm. He'll be back soon."

On seeing the farmhouse, Jimmy stopped, stood a moment, and let his eyes travel over the porch, the second-floor windows and roof, the trees. He took it all in, and swallowed.

"It's good to be home."

As he walked up the steps, he glanced at the banner in the window – a gold star at the top with three blue stars beneath it. Next to it was the Illinois Silver Star emblem with the words: *Our Home Has Contributed*. He turned away.

"Come! Come inside!" said Kate, running up the steps. "Ursula, boil some water. We'll make coffee. Jessica, take the pumpkin pie out of the pantry. Oh, the house is a mess! It's wash day and we were just finishing up. There's clothing all over the place!"

Before the front door closed, Ursula briefly glanced towards the barn. She saw that Friedrich was helping Karl and Otto carry the tools into the machine shed. She tried to catch his eye, but the others were there, and he wouldn't look her way. A pang shot through her; she hadn't heard what he was about to say. She had forgotten everything in her joy at seeing Jimmy. What was it he was going to tell her?

Kate bustled around the kitchen, trying to do a hundred things at once for her son's comfort. She reached for his coat, but he took if off and hung it on the hall tree. She pulled out the chair for him to sit, and then smoothed back his hair and kissed his forehead.

"Have you had lunch? Shall I fix you a sandwich? Or how about – "

Jimmy held up his hand. "Don't fuss, Mom. I can wait for dinner. Though some coffee and a piece of pie sounds mighty good."

While Ursula prepared the coffee and Jessica sliced a piece of pie for him, Jimmy walked from room to room, as if refreshing his memory, or reacquainting himself with his home.

Kate followed him, watching his face, trying to see it through his eyes.

"Boy, am I glad to be home." He hugged his mother and lifted her off her feet.

Kate laughed in protest. "Put me down before you hurt yourself."

Arm in arm, they walked back into the kitchen and sat down at the table.

Jessica set the pie in front of him and pulled her chair close to his. "First, Paul in the spring, and now you. Two brothers in one year! Who could have guessed?"

Kate jumped up and went into the living room, calling out behind her. "We just had a letter from Paul. He's in Australia! Here's his letter," she said, handing a single page to Jimmy.

He briefly scanned the letter. "Not much of a letter writer, is he?"

"You can talk," teased Jessica.

"I know, I know. I never have much to say, but I love getting your letters." Jimmy more carefully looked at the changes in his sisters.

"Look at you two. All grown up. You've put on a little weight, Ursula, since last time I saw you."

Ursula blushed crimson and was about to speak but Jimmy put up a hand.

"No, you look good. I was afraid you were going to remain scrawny all your life, like Jessica here."

Jessica gave him a light smack on his shoulder. "I've gained weight, too. In spite of the rationing, Ursula and I have managed to gain a few pounds. Scrawny, indeed!"

He playfully held up his hands for cover. "You both look good. And Mom, you look exactly the same."

Jimmy folded the letter and slid it back into the envelope, and then examined the photograph of Paul.

Kate smiled down at the image of her youngest son.

"Doesn't he look older?" She leaned over and hugged Jimmy again. "Oh, I can't wait to have you all home again. All together again." Her voice began to quiver, and she went to the pantry. She took a moment, and then came back with a tin of biscuits and set it in front of Jimmy.

"Now, you can't spoil me while I'm home. You'll make me soft and then I won't be fit for duty," he said, taking a biscuit.

He stirred some sugar into his cup, took a sip, and then took a few bites of pie. He let out a deep sigh. "Home cooking. Nothing beats it." He took another bite, then reached down to his duffle bag and opened it. "Now. First things first." He rummaged through it, pulled out a bag, and set it on the table.

Jessica sat up in expectation and exchanged a look of delight with Ursula.

Jimmy first took out a small box and handed it to his mother.

Kate opened the velvet box and put her hand to her heart. "Oh!" She lifted out a brooch, a swirl of sparkling blue stones. "Oh, Jimmy!" She held it out for her daughters to see. "Just look at that."

Then he handed out embroidered handkerchiefs for them all, and chocolates.

After a little more rummaging around in his bag, he pulled out three boxes in different colors – pink, purple, and pale yellow, covered in embossed flowers. He handed one to each of them.

"Soap!" squealed Jessica. "Real soap." She opened her box. "Oh, look, they're wrapped in matching paper. How beautiful!" She brought it to her nose and inhaled. "Ahh! Mine's honeysuckle. What's yours, Mom?"

Kate handed her the pink box. "Rose. Just smell that – like a breath of summer."

"And mine's lilac," said Ursula, passing the purple box around. "Thank you, Jimmy!"

"In every letter Jessica sent she complained about the homemade soap, so I thought I'd better not come home without some."

"I only wrote that once!" Jessica protested. "Maybe twice."

"James," chided Kate. "You shouldn't be spending all your money on such extravagant gifts for us."

"Why not? Who else am I going to spend it on?"

Jessica leaned forward. "You mean you don't have a girl?"

"I did. When I was stationed in San Diego. For about a month. But she dumped me for a jar head. Then I had another girl in Hawaii. A real sweetie. But – I don't know. Neither one of us wanted to get serious. And then – "

"Jimmy!" Ursula said with a laugh. "You always had a way with the girls."

"I met a girl on the train. Carol. No, Cora. Sat next to her all the way from Chi-town." He took a bite of pie and made sounds of enjoyment. "What about you two? Ursula? You got a fella? Is Joe Madden still sweet on you?"

"Joe finally gave up on Ursula," said Jessica. "He's engaged to Sue Ellen!"

Jimmy almost choked on his coffee. "Dang, he's even braver than I thought. Sue Ellen'll talk his ear off every night." With mock incrimination, he turned to Ursula. "You drove him to this?"

Ursula had to laugh. "Joe and I were just friends. That's all we ever were. And Sue Ellen will make him happy."

"I know you got someone," Jimmy persisted. "As soon as I saw you, I thought – "

Ursula jumped up. "Don't be ridiculous." She brought the coffee pot to the table and topped up his cup.

Jessica gave a sly glance at Ursula. "She swears she doesn't have a beau. But she *has* been spending a suspicious amount of time up in Peoria with her friend Dolores."

"Dolores? The one with all the brothers? It's about time you had a fella. Is he a soldier?"

"Don't rush her," said Kate. "She's determined to attend college. This war can't last forever."

"All the same, a gal needs a fella to go to parties and dances with, or write letters to if he's overseas."

Jessica leaned forward. "Speaking of parties and dances, the Bloomfields are having a Christmas party. And there's the Christmas dance in town. And guess what? Gladys Wilkins is back working at the dry goods store. She's there every Saturday."

"Is that so?" Jimmy smiled.

"And she asks about you every single time we go in there. Though she's still kind of shy."

"I'll have to stop by. Check out the lay of the land. And I won't be missing any of the dances or parties. Gotta get my fill while I can."

He leaned back in his chair. "And I got a lot of plans for when I'm home. I want to fix the place up a bit. Not that it needs it, but I can't be bested by my little brother. Paul went on and on about the picket fence he made, and the new coat of paint on the house. I can't let him outdo me. I'm going to build a swinging gate for the fence. And an archway for your garden like you've always wanted, and – "

They heard a truck door slam, and then footsteps hurrying to the porch. Soon the kitchen door opened.

"Ed!" Jimmy cried, and ran to embrace the old farm hand.

On seeing the tears in the old man's eyes, Jimmy began to choke up. "God dang! You're all going to have me crying before the day's out." He draped his arm around Ed's shoulder. "Come and sit down, Ed. How the heck are you? How's Opal?"

Ursula and Jessica soon had a cup of coffee and a slice of pie set in front of Ed.

Ed took off his hat and hung it on the back of his chair. He couldn't stop smiling. "Opal's fine. She'll be glad to hear you're home. So, how's life on board an aircraft carrier? Can't even imagine what that's like."

They all listened rapt while Jimmy recounted some of his experiences in the Pacific. "Though there are plenty of days when it's the boredom that nearly kills us. Just waiting for orders."

"But it's better than the Aleutians?" asked Jessica.

Jimmy placed his head in his hands and groaned. "Anyplace is better than that hell hole. Barren, soggy, gale one moment, sunshine the next. Then a storm."

"What was it you'd tell the newcomers?" asked Jessica. "'If you don't like the weather, just wait a minute.'"

Jimmy grinned at the memory. He took the last bite of his pie and pushed his plate away. "At least there's sunshine in the Pacific."

Kate suddenly got up from her chair. "Look at the time! I need to get dinner started or we won't be eating until midnight. Jimmy, I'll make you a pot roast tomorrow, but for tonight, how about some fried chicken?"

"With mashed potatoes and gravy," added Jessica, also jumping to her feet.

"Can't think of anything I'd rather have. Ed, why don't you show me around the farm, show me what needs fixing while I'm home. It all looks just like I remember – but I sure don't like the idea of a bunch of Krauts here on our farm."

Kate walked with him to the door. "We're lucky to have them, Jimmy. I don't know what we would have done without them. They're good men. All three of them."

"The only good Kraut is a dead Kraut," Jimmy said, placing his cap on his head.

Ed slipped on his jacket. "Let's go before it gets dark. I'll show you the new fencing along the pasture. And the shelving in the machine shed that Paul built in the spring. Don't know why we never thought of it before."

Ursula watched them through the window. Otto came out of the barn and shook Jimmy's hand, and then pointed to the POWs. Ursula saw that he introduced the men, for Gustav smiled and extended his hand. But Jimmy didn't take it. He stood a moment, and then moved towards the pasture with Ed.

Ursula went to the sink and began to scrub the potatoes Jessica had just dumped in. Kate remained looking out the window. "I hope he doesn't say anything," she said quietly. Then louder, "I think I'll go out and walk with them." Kate took off her apron, slipped on her jacket, and left to catch up with them.

"Mom's going to make sure Jimmy doesn't say anything," said Jessica. "They're all so sad. About Friedrich's news."

Ursula whipped around. "What news?"

Jessica stared at her with wide eyes. "I thought you knew. I thought that's why you were so quiet. When you were in Peoria we found out, but I thought –"

"What? What news?"

"He got a letter. From someone he knows in Germany. His home, the whole town, was destroyed in a bombing raid two months ago."

The color left Ursula's face. She waited for more information.

"It killed everyone," Jessica said softly. "His mother, his sister and her children. It's terrible. No one wants to talk about it. It's too sad."

Jessica heard Otto's pickup truck and went to the window. "They're heading back to camp. Just as well. It'll take Jimmy some time to get used to the idea of them being here."

Ursula's hands were shaking as she dropped the potatoes and brush in the sink, and then left the room.

Christmastime 1944

Chapter 5

Charles lay in the Bethesda Naval Hospital diagnosed with another case of pneumonia. His spirits sank when he was given the diagnosis. He knew he was run down, but had hoped it wasn't pneumonia again. The doctor told him that the dangerous bout he had the previous year had most likely weakened his lungs. There was no immediate danger, but he could not be released until the penicillin worked its magic. Which meant a delay in getting home.

Penicillin. The drug that had saved so many lives. He knew he wouldn't be here now if it weren't for the drug. It had saved his life when he languished in Cairo last year.

He would have to tell Lillian. She would be worried sick and would try to come down. He would prefer that she didn't know – but she was so angry last year when the truth came out as to why he hadn't been able to come home for Christmas.

He had kept so much from her, and again this year. He had to. He couldn't talk of the war. So instead he wrote about the time spent in port, the brief four-hour runs ashore.

And yet he should have been more honest with her. Told her that he had been ill. Or had he told her? Was that the cause of their argument? No. It was something about a baby. Lillian wanted a baby. He realized his mind was wandering, cloudy moments alongside clear memories. It must be the fever. He rubbed his temples and wiped the sweat from his face.

He closed his eyes and listened to the absence of sounds in the hospital, the stillness. No rolling and pitching underfoot. No crash of waves against the ship, no North Atlantic gales with thirty-foot waves. He had served in the Great War. But he didn't remember the feeling of horror, the claustrophobia of being four decks down, knowing that if they were struck all the watertight hatches would prevent him from escaping, the cold water finding its way in…

He snapped his eyes open and listened. So quiet now. No bells or whistles or alarms jarring him out of sleep. No explosions when a torpedo hit its mark, or a ship in convoy hit a mine. Snow that should have been white – black, sooty, greasy.

No – that was last winter, off Iceland. Everything was blending together. The mine was this summer. He tried not to remember the men being blown into the air, parts of them landing in the water in the steel and wood and dirty foam. The stench of oil and human flesh. The casualties. Casualties. Who came up with that word? So offhand, so incidental. So far from the truth. Perhaps it was supposed to be causalities. Someone made a simple mistake. No. That didn't make sense either. He rubbed his face. No point in trying to make sense of the senseless. He jolted up, overtaken by an eruption of coughing, and then collapsed into exhaustion.

"Mr. Drooms?" Someone touched his arm.

He gasped in fear – then remembered where he was.

It was the nurse, lightly shaking him awake. "I have your medicine, and we'll try a vapor treatment, shall we? That should ease your breathing."

All this cleanliness and cheerfulness. He didn't quite trust it. A quick remedy to patch him up for the next battle, and the next…

No. She was a kind nurse. He was in the States. He was sure of it. And now, he could breath. While the vapor treatment lasted, he felt good – the ease of breathing. Like the harbor breeze in Alexandria, so mild, so sweet…

He must have dozed off after the treatment. When he awoke, he felt somewhat better. He picked up the letters from Lillian, and Tommy and Gabriel, intending to read them again. There was something he wasn't clear about, some shadow that lurked in the letters. Several times Gabriel had mentioned a man. Henry. Who worked with Lillian.

Charles sifted through the letters, then set them back down. Later. They would require stamina that he didn't have right now. Later. He would make sense of everything later.

He looked at the time. The nurse said it would be an hour before he could have the dose of medicine that would help him sleep. That would take away the visions that kept creeping into his mind. The humiliations that were rumored to take place in the prison camps – he couldn't bear to repeat them to himself. He could never tell Lillian. The wounded. The senselessness of death. Poor Michael Barlow. So optimistic, so happy to be getting married. Was going to teach history. Yes. That's what had brought them together, Classical history, ancient Rome. Several conversations. Michael, too, had studied history and literature, seeking out what was good and noble. It had helped him, too.

But now? He was overwhelmed by mankind's capacity for cruelty, the sickening hunger for revenge. The horror of it all. He felt his mind moving towards a vision he didn't want to see. He wanted to think of good things, but he forgot what they were.

And there it was – in front of him, again. Sharp. Fresh. The night along the Dalmatian coast, on watch with young Michael, watching a battle from afar. From a safe distance, he had thought. Michael talking about marrying his girl on his next leave, and how they had met at a dance. How he wasn't much of a dancer and had stepped on her toe – twice! And still she danced with him. Michael laughed at the memory, lit a cigarette, and said he couldn't wait to get back home, and take her dancing again. They were standing there, eyes on the coast, laughing at his story – and the next moment – Michael's head was blown off. He was still standing, but headless.

Charles rubbed at his face, chasing the vision away. He had seen so much horror, but that…

Something had happened inside him. He realized there was no dignity in death. No meaning.

He pushed himself up on his pillow, took a sip of water, and tried to keep his mind on now. Here. He was in a U.S. hospital. Getting better. He looked around at the lumps in the other beds in the ward. I guess this is what they call depression, he thought. Or battle fatigue? I must snap out of it. I can't bring this home to Lillian.

Lillian. He looked at the pile of letters that had awaited him when he arrived. And a history book that someone had brought for him. He must have said something to someone about Roman history. But he would not read the book. For the truth was, there never was a time of peace. There was no Pax Romana. History was just one long bloody battle. Full of sulphurous smoke and deafening sound. Like Vesuvius, the underlying violence in all of nature.

He coughed up his sickness, dripping in sweat, and fell back onto his pillow. What we should be repulsed by, we instead embrace, and madness descends upon the world. And we are dragged down. Red in tooth and claw – was that Darwin? Tennyson? He forgot who came first, he couldn't remember the poems, the lore, the beautiful words. They were all jumbled in the black oily water strewn with bodies in the long bloated nightmare of war.

He hated it. He hated it and didn't want to go back. He turned his head from side to side, trying to get away from it. It's the fever. It must be the fever. These were not his normal thoughts.

Were they? A wracking cough so sharp he thought his ribs would crack.

A cool cloth. "Here we go," said the nurse.

The liquid burned his throat and stopped the spasms. Now he would sleep, and the visions would stop. Now there would be room in his mind for Lillian. Her sweet voice. Her soft touch. She would never leave him, would she? Would she? He heard a sob break from his chest and he felt wetness in his eyes.

His breathing eased, the fire cooled. He would keep Lillian cradled in his mind. Sleeping in her arms. But who was Henry? He softly slid into dark, velvety sleep; but a troubling image followed him there – that of Lillian letting go of his hand and walking away from him.

*

Lillian had met with the drama teacher earlier in the week and was relieved to hear that there were plenty of volunteers for sewing costumes and painting backdrops. All she had to do was provide some drawings, something she could do at home in the evenings. A Christmas village scene for one skit, a few costume designs for fairies and elves and snow maidens, and a backdrop or two for the play the kids were writing. She was looking forward to working so freely, without restrictions from Rockwell or the Office of War Information. Perhaps she could add some of these drawings to her portfolio for her meeting with Mrs. Huntington.

Everything seemed to be coming together. She had come a long way from working as a department store clerk when she first moved to New York City. She had later taken a job as a switchboard operator at Rockwell Publishing, working her way up to the position of a senior illustrator in the Art Department. Now, it looked as if she was getting even closer to her old dream of being a freelance artist, with more freedom in depicting the subjects that meant most to her.

Lillian glanced at the clock. The children would be arriving any moment. While they worked on the play, she would use the time to go through her portfolio. In between stirring a pan of hot chocolate, she arranged a plate of oatmeal cookies, and took several mugs from the cupboard. She looked out over the apartment, glad that she had put out a few decorations, even though Christmas was still weeks away. A garland hung from the mantel, beneath pinecone trees and several of the Victorian postcards she set out every year – images of holly and mistletoe, and children ice skating, sledding, and carrying gifts.

She smiled on hearing footsteps and laughter coming up the stairs. Always so full of energy. Gabriel threw open the door, followed by Billy, Mickey, Tommy, and Amy.

They were quick to spot the cookies and as they greeted Lillian, they gathered around the coffee table.

"Your mom always has good food," observed Billy, crunching into a cookie and then theatrically lying on the floor to express just how good it was.

Though Billy always had a way of making her laugh, Lillian secretly worried about the combination of him and Gabriel together in the play. She hoped their antics wouldn't derail the seriousness of the play.

"And I made some hot chocolate for you while you work on your script," said Lillian.

"Do we have marshmallows?" asked Tommy.

"Yes, we do. I'll bring you all a cup."

Amy was immediately by her side. "I'll help."

Mickey and Tommy spread out their notes while Amy and Lillian set mugs of hot chocolate in front of them.

Amy took her hot chocolate and stood in front of the mantel, admiring Lillian's arrangement. "I just love your old-fashioned cards, Mrs. Drooms. The clothes were so pretty back then, weren't they?" She dipped her head to one side. "Do you only collect cards with little girls in them?"

"Why no, I – " Lillian looked at the dozen cards she had chosen out of about thirty. Sure enough – they were all of little girls.

"Well, isn't that odd?" she said, puzzling over her choice of cards. Strange that she should –

Tommy looked up. "Mom, we asked Mrs. Kuntzman if we could interview her and she said yes, *and* she said that we could have our meetings at her place."

"Oh, I don't want you to impose on her."

"She really wants to," said Gabriel. "She said she'll have treats and can answer our questions. And she said to bring Henry. 'The more, the merrier.' That's what she said." Gabriel clasped his hands, perfectly capturing the charm of Mrs. Kuntzman.

"'It vill be a leetle party. Give me chance to cook for someone, now youse boys too old for babysitter.'"

Lillian smiled, and understood that the boys' babysitter of the past four years missed seeing them on a regular basis. They only went to her if Lillian knew she had to work into the evening and would be late for dinner, which was always a treat for the boys.

"So, we're going to her place on Thursday to interview her and Henry."

Lillian took her portfolio to the kitchen table and began sorting through her work. But she soon became engrossed in their conversation, observing the differences between them all. She made quick sketches of them as they raised questions and decided on plot points.

They went over the action, with Mickey reading what they had so far, including brief character descriptions. In addition to being the director, Amy would play the wife in the final scene, and a few younger students would play her sons and daughters. Mickey would play the wounded WWI soldier, and Tommy would be his commanding officer. Billy would have a few bit parts: the German soldier in no-man's-land, and the fisherman towards the end of the play. He would also be in charge of sound effects, which he was demonstrating to Gabriel's great enjoyment.

Billy stood in the middle of the room, as if on stage. "And here's what I have in mind for the Jerry who gets bayonetted." He enacted a dramatic death scene, which caused Gabriel to howl with amusement. Billy then mimed what he imagined to be a French fisherman, motoring his boat, cutting the engine, and then throwing a line over the side – and immediately hooking a large, slippery fish that eventually pulled him overboard.

"You're not going to have time for all that," his older brother, Mickey, protested. "And you can't overdo it. It's not supposed to be funny."

"Okay, so I'll tone it down." Billy mimed using a smaller pole and catching a smaller fish.

"We still need a role for me," Gabriel reminded them. "I don't want to be Jerry Number Two in no-man's-land – he doesn't have any lines."

"Gabriel's right," said Amy. "The plot was his idea, so he needs a good part."

"How about the ghost of his friend?"

"We decided – no ghosts," said Tommy. "There's no time for it. It's already way too long. We can't add more roles."

"How about the captain of the ship that picks him up?" suggested Billy.

"That happens off-stage," said Tommy. "We could add a second fisherman."

"Nah," said Gabriel.

"How about a farmer at the end?"

Gabriel frowned at the idea.

"I have it!" cried Amy, jumping to her feet. "You can open and close the play! With a prologue and epilogue! My mom took me to see *Rom* – a Shakespeare play this summer, and there was a guy who came out and told everyone what the play was going to be about and then made a comment at the end."

"What was the play?" asked Tommy.

"Something with a lot of fighting in it," said Amy, causing Lillian to smile.

Tommy sat up. "That's a great idea. Gabriel can tell the audience exactly where and when it takes place and what's going on. That'll save us time, too.

"That'll solve a lot of our problems," said Mickey. "How about it Gabriel?"

"Hmm," he said, rubbing his chin, Henry-like. "Could be interesting. What about a costume?"

"You could be a Father Time sort of character," said Amy, "or a WWI soldier – a doughboy."

"Or Father Christmas," offered Billy. "Or all three."

"What will I say?" asked Gabriel.

"You'll set the scene and describe the basic plot," said Tommy.

Mickey was writing down the ideas as fast as he could. "And at the end you can say a few words about war and Christmas."

"And say something nice at the very end," said Billy. "Like Tiny Tim." He spoke out of one side of his mouth in a cockney accent so thick he could barely be understood. "'God bless us. Everyone!'"

Tommy looked slightly worried as he watched Billy. "Or maybe just wish everyone a Merry Christmas. Keep it simple."

"And we'll write it in poetic language, so it really stands out," added Amy. "Let's all bring some ideas and lines of poetry to work on next time. This is going to be great!"

"We'll ask Henry for some ideas on Thursday," suggested Gabriel. "He'll have some real humdingers. Some real doozies!"

Tommy groaned and realized that letting Gabriel have the final lines could be a big mistake. "You can't mess up, Gabriel. Especially with the ending. It wraps up the play, so it's really important." He turned to Amy. "Maybe it's not such a good idea."

"Think you can memorize poetic lines, Gabe?" asked Mickey.

"Sure."

"Or," said Amy, holding her finger up, "we could make a scroll and you could read the Prologue, or refer to it if you forget. Like a prop. And we'll keep the Epilogue short and sweet – easy to remember. Our time will be up, and everyone will want to have punch and snacks by then. One line, and then *Merry Christmas!* Something like that."

"Swell!" said Gabriel. "That'll leave more time for acting. I think I'll be a wounded Father Christmas from the Great War." He brought his mug to the kitchen table, dragging his leg behind him.

"We'll work out the details later," said Tommy, cracking his knuckles.

"Hey!" said Billy. "You can use the robe from my Grim Reaper costume I made for Halloween. Maybe we can add some holly or bells to make it look like Christmas. I have a book of Christmas stories with pictures that might help."

"And I have a book on the Great War," said Mickey. "Maybe we can get some ideas for costumes and stuff. Let's go take a look!"

They all jumped to their feet, fired up at the idea. "Mom," cried Tommy, "we're running to Mickey's to look at some books. Then you can draw up the costumes."

They pulled on their coats, grabbed a few more cookies, and dashed out the door.

"All right," Lillian called after them. "But I want you home in an hour!"

She closed the door on the small whirlwind, smiling at their exuberance. She made herself a cup of tea, and brought her portfolio to the coffee table. She took the last cookie and bit into it, and then began to flip through her drawings.

She worried that she didn't have enough work to show Mrs. Huntington, but as she began to look through her drawings, she was amazed at the quantity. There had been countless campaigns and the need for posters and magazine illustrations was endless.

She realized that her portfolio largely chronicled the war. "Bundles for America," depicting kits full of shaving cream, toothpaste and brushes, soap, sewing kits. The posters for book drives: "Books for Victory," "Books for Buddies," "We Want Books." Several posters each year for war bonds: she flipped to her first ones in 1942, showing that one 10 cent stamp would pay for 5 bullets, 25 cents would pay for a soldier's mess kit, and $1.50 in stamps would pay for a first aid kit. She lifted a poster from the Fifth War Bond Drive from the summer that depicted a working woman purchasing a bond.

Here was a poster to raise funds for high school classes to purchase and then build model airplanes for the civil defense spotters. Fifty different models of American and Axis planes. And posters for all the paper and metal drives. She held up a drawing for a rubber drive, with images of garden hoses, dolls, girdles, raincoats, galoshes, and door mats.

Many posters were targeted to housewives, as with the collection of nylons and silk stockings, and grease. She smiled at the picture of a stout housewife participating in the Fats Salvage: first, an image of her scraping kitchen fats into an old coffee can, and then selling them to the local butcher – to be collected and then used for making dynamite and TNT. Other illustrations called on women to knit articles for military personnel, and sew garments for hospitals and surgical dressings for the Red Cross. Here was a sketch that was never used: a coffee rationing poster from last summer, just before the rationing for it ended.

Drawing after drawing. She had to ask herself – If it weren't for the war, would I have produced so much? Or would I have doodled away the years, starting drawings but not completing them, wishing to live the life of an artist, but not doing anything about it? The war had toughened her, in a good way. It had forced her to be her best, to push her limits, to produce more than she had ever thought possible. It was as if she had tapped into an unlimited pool of ideas and energy. She held up one of the drawings from the Milkweed Campaign.

My expertise on a weed, indeed! Her anger flared at Rockwell's comment. He had diminished her efforts, all those extra hours she had put in to make the Milkweed Campaign a success. She had won some recognition for it, and was proud of the campaign, but it had not gone to her head, as Rockwell claimed.

Lillian took a sip of tea and tucked her legs underneath her, remembering the urgent meeting at the end of spring announcing the new campaign. It began with Rockwell striding into the conference room, enjoying his sense of importance, and introducing the government officials.

"This is Mr. Roberts and Miss Mills, representatives from the Milkweed Floss Division of the War Hemp Industries."

Lillian had sat first in disbelief, and then in amusement, at the importance being given to a weed.

"Posters for this campaign must be delivered in time for the schoolyear," said Rockwell. "So, you don't got much time. Mr. Roberts'll fill you in."

"Good morning. As you all know, Japan has invaded the Dutch East Indies, and along with our supply of rubber, they have cut off our supply of *kapok*. Kapoc, also known as Java Cotton, is used for life vests, and as insulation for flight suits. A potentially dire predicament," he added dramatically. He looked out at the group and waited for his words to register. Then he held up a finger and smiled. "Fortunately, we have discovered that the common milkweed has similar properties: it is lightweight and buoyant, as the floss is hollow and covered in wax."

The artists exchanged glances, wondering where he was going with this information.

"We need vast quantities, vast!" he said, with his arms outspread. "Unfortunately, this would take three years to grow commercially." Again, his index finger shot up. "So, we're going to harvest our floss from a crop that is already mature and grows in abundance, from Canada to Georgia. But it must be harvested before the pods burst in the fall. Hence the urgency of our campaign."

An older artist raised his hand. "Who will gather this – crop?"

"Excellent question! With most of the nation already employed, or indeed, enlisted, we will use students to gather the pods, much as we use the Boy Scouts to disseminate posters on information for the war effort. The students will collect them in September, before the pods open. In particular, we'll target the junior high schools. So, it's of the utmost importance that the posters appeal to that age group. I'm sure there are mothers and father, aunts and uncles among you. Perhaps you can be at the forefront of this campaign."

A young woman sitting across from Lillian raised her hand. "Excuse me, sir. I was born and raised in the city and don't even know what one looks like."

"We'll issue photographs and samples, and slogans for you to base your drawings on. For example: 'Two bags save one life.' Catchy, isn't it? Is anyone here familiar with the plant?"

When his question was met with silence and looks at one another around the table, Lillian tentatively spoke up. "I was raised upstate and am familiar with it. It grew all along the roadside and fences." Lillian turned to the other artists. "In the fall it releases a silky white floss that the wind then carries along – kind of like cottonwood trees, or dandelions." Lillian grew more animated as the artists began to show interest. "It's considered a weed, though we had an old neighbor who said the Indians, the Iroquois, I believe, used it as both food and medicine. And he said it's essential to the monarch butterfly. It's actually a rather interesting plant – "

Rockwell grunted and addressed Mr. Roberts. "This is Mrs. Drooms, and since she knows so much about the weed, she'll be in charge of the campaign."

Lillian flushed and wished she had kept her mouth shut. She didn't know anything about running campaigns. Was Rockwell punishing her? Or testing her? Her mettle rose. "Of course, Mr. Rockwell. I'd be delighted."

Mr. Roberts nodded. "Wonderful. We'll meet with you after the meeting to give you the details and timeline." He turned to his assistant. "Miss Mills, the exhibits, please."

Miss Mills opened a case and passed around samples of milkweed pods and floss, and then held up a large netted bag in each hand.

One of the women showed her surprise at the exhibit. "Why, those look like – "

"Onion bags," smiled Mr. Roberts. "Precisely. Onion bags, such as these, will be provided by the government for the collection of pods. They are light weight, and will aid in the process of drying."

At first Lillian had been angry with Rockwell, though in retrospect, it was an opportunity that she would never have asked for on her own. He must have known that she was capable; he would never risk a losing proposition. She supposed she should be grateful. Yes, she thought, straightening her shoulders. She would use her management of the campaign in her interview with Mrs. Huntington, to demonstrate her ability. Thank you, Mr. Rockwell!

She looked at several drawings she had submitted, three of which were among the key posters used for the campaign, which had been a great success. The children took to the task and made a game of it. Kate had written that their town had met their quota early. And Jessica, as part of her training for becoming a teacher, had supervised several outings, one of them along the railroad, and another one right on their farm. Kate wrote that the children arrived early, brought their onion bags, and Jessica took them along the roads and fences where the plant grew in abundance. They had a picnic lunch, and gathered the pods until it was nearly dark, making an adventure of it.

Lillian remembered how she began the first meeting of the campaign with a quote from Emerson: "A weed is a plant whose virtues have not yet been discovered." She studied a few of her drawings of the humble milkweed and thought how like people they were – often undervalued or underestimated. Without the war effort, how many such people would have gone unnoticed? Women, the handicapped, children, the elderly – everyone had value that often went unrecognized.

In her heart, Lillian believed the reason her milkweed posters had turned out so well was because of her affection for the unassuming plant and its fairylike beauty. As girls, she and her sister Annette had ridden their bikes along the country roads, delighting in the milkweed. They would crack open the rough-looking pods and slide the silky floss between their fingers, and then release it in the late-summer breeze. There was something utterly magical about the plant.

She smiled at the drawing she had not submitted, in which fairy-like creatures floated along with the milkweed floss. Her mind always pulled her in the direction of make-believe and fancy, of unreality, and dreams – a tendency she hid at Rockwell Publishing. Perhaps if she worked as a freelance artist, it might serve as a strength. She would add the sketch to her portfolio.

But now, for her first meeting with Mrs. Huntington, she needed to emphasize the practical skills she had learned from her years at Rockwell Publishing, and present herself as professional and capable. It had taken her years to develop her skills and perfect her techniques. But it had all been worthwhile; she was now utterly confident that her work had value and was marketable – and the art director from a publishing company wanted to meet with her! And she was ready.

Christmastime 1944

Chapter 6

ᕽ

Ursula stood at her bedroom window, a shawl wrapped around her nightgown, waiting for the first glimmer of dawn. She parted the lace curtains and gazed out at the dark sky. She had barely slept. Her heart ached for Friedrich, for how terrible his world had become. He was utterly alone. A prisoner far from home. Last year his brother had been killed in Stalingrad. And now – his entire family, gone. His home destroyed. His past, his roots, the place and people of his memories – gone.

Then she had the terrible thought – what if it had been Eugene's plane that dropped the bomb? Was Friedrich wondering the same thing? Would his loss change his feelings for her? But perhaps the Germans had killed or captured Eugene. Would that change her feelings for Friedrich? No. Nothing would ever change her heart towards him.

No wonder he had looked different, more worn, bereft. She remembered the anger in his eyes, then the haunted emptiness that filled them when he was about to tell her of his loss. And she had run away in joy at the sight of Jimmy.

And now Friedrich had doubt in his mind as to why she went to Peoria. She had to clear things up, and let him know that he was not alone, and that she would never leave him.

She dressed and went downstairs to start preparing breakfast. The others would be up soon. Chores needed to be done, the animals needed tending. She would keep busy until Friedrich arrived.

Though Kate had tried to dissuade Jimmy from working while he was home, he was eager to get started on his projects. Over breakfast he and Kate discussed the plans for the day, deciding that they would get started on the ditches while the weather was mild. Ursula's heart sank. That meant Friedrich would be gone all day. When she heard Otto's truck arrive with the POWs, her mind raced. It would take them a while to load up. She topped up Jimmy's cup of coffee and her own, and then made another pot.

She would risk Jimmy's disapproval and bring out a thermos of coffee to the prisoners before they left. It would provide a thin excuse for why she was out there, if someone should ask.

She busied herself in the kitchen where she could see out the window into the farmyard. Jessica came down, ready for school, and sat at the table. Jimmy questioned her about her classes, and who was teaching which subjects. Kate had gone outside to discuss the day's plans with Ed and Otto.

Soon the POWs were loading up the truck with the tools they would need. When Ursula saw Friedrich go alone to the machine shed, she took the thermos and stacked some cups and stepped outside.

She glanced behind her before entering the machine shed and looked around inside. They were alone. "Friedrich," she said softly. She set the thermos and cups on the shelves.

He lifted a shovel down from the hooks on the wall, and turned to her.

She walked up to him and placed her hand on his arm. "I'm so sorry. I didn't know. I only found out yesterday." She was about to take his hand, when she became aware of someone entering. She drew away, fearing it was Jimmy.

"Need a hand?" asked Ed. He came inside and took one of the shovels Friedrich had taken down. "Mornin', Ursula."

"Morning, Ed," she replied, reaching for the thermos. "How about some coffee?"

He shook his head. "Where's that sleepy-headed brother of yours?" Ed asked, loud enough so that Jimmy overhead him as he walked into the shed. Ursula sensed that Ed was giving her warning. Had Ed seen her hand on Friedrich's arm?

"I was up with the dawn, as you well know," said Jimmy. "Feeding and watering the animals. And ready to work." His smile dropped when he faced Friedrich. "I'll take that." He grabbed the shovel away from Friedrich.

Friedrich bristled at the rudeness of Jimmy's manner.

"Let's get started then," Ed said, leading the way to the barn.

Ursula felt the hostility between Friedrich and Jimmy. She grabbed Jimmy's arm. "Mom said you're going to start on the ditches?"

"Ed and I are. I'm not working with German scum."

When they reached the barn, Jimmy scowled. There was Otto chuckling at one of Karl's stories, and Jessica stood next to Gustav, cooing at the photographs in his hands.

"Here, Otto – freshly made," said Ursula, handing him a cup of coffee. She poured another cup and set it next to Gustav. Jimmy's eyes narrowed in anger.

Gustav nodded his thanks and said softly, "*Danke.*"

Jessica took one of the photographs to show to Ursula. "Oh, look at this! Gustav has photos of – "

"Jessica!" scolded Jimmy.

Her head snapped up at his accusatory tone. "What?" She looked from Jimmy to Ursula. Ursula gave a slight shake of her head.

"Gustav is just showing me his pictures. They just arrived yesterday. His sons and – "

Ursula put her arm around her sister. "Hurry, Jessica. There's the bus."

Jessica groaned. "It's not fair! My brother finally comes home and I have to go to school."

Jimmy forced a grin. "Still the same. You just hate to miss out on anything." He walked her outside the barn. "If you want to be a teacher you better get to school and keep learning. As I recall, your math was never too good. I'll be here a whole month, Jess. Go on."

He watched Jessica run down the lane to the bus, and then he came back inside and stood next to Ursula. He watched her hand a cup of coffee to Karl.

Jimmy couldn't contain his outrage. "Don't they get coffee at camp? Everyone knows they're better fed than the rest of us."

Ursula ignored his remark and handed the cup to Karl, who looked up, not quite catching what Jimmy was saying, but aware of his disapproval.

"Ed," said Jimmy, keeping his eyes fixed on the prisoners, "have you heard about the camp for Nazi officers down in Mississippi?"

"Can't say as I have," said Ed, uncomfortable with Jimmy's tone.

"They call it the Fritz Ritz. Private bungalows, valets, gardens, wine..."

"I find that hard to believe," said Ursula, pouring out a cup for Friedrich.

"It's true, all right. Just ask Otto."

Ursula handed the cup to Friedrich, but he raised his palm in refusal, his eyes on Jimmy.

Otto pushed at the straw by his feet. "Well, I heard about that camp – it's for the generals. Some folks are pretty upset about it. But others point out that we gotta follow the Geneva Convention. And it'll increase the chances our boys will be treated well over there."

Jimmy spat at the idea. "Our men are starving, treated like dogs. I can't begin to tell you the stories we hear. The Germans are brutes. Arrogant brutes. We don't need to waste our coffee on such swine."

Otto subtly motioned to the POWs. Gustav and Karl understood that Jimmy's angry words concerned them, and moved outside. But Friedrich stood still, and held Jimmy's gaze.

Ed stepped up between them. "Truth is, Jimmy, everyone works better with a little hot food and coffee inside them. You know that. And we have a lot of work ahead of us. Let's get goin'."

Ursula set the cup down, alarmed by Jimmy's hostility. She could see that Friedrich was seething inside. Otto took his arm and said something in German and Friedrich reluctantly followed him outside.

"I don't like the insolence in that one," said Jimmy.

"Then stop provoking him, and let them get on with their chores," Ursula snapped. She turned and left the barn.

Ed walked up to Jimmy. "You gotta remember, we're still runnin' a farm here. We need their help. I know it's hard for you, but everything's all twisted and backwards these days and we just have to work with what we got."

Jimmy watched Ed go out and speak to Otto, and come back.

"Otto'll take the boys on down to the creek, get started on the trees. Got several days' worth of work. Keep 'em outta your hair. Come on, Jimmy. You and me'll work on the ditches in the south field. Should be done by noon if we start now."

Jimmy's face showed repugnance as he watched Otto explain the change in plans.

"And what the heck's wrong with Otto, acting like he's one of them. He's supposed to be guarding them. He doesn't even have a gun!"

"He's been working here with these three for over a year. Truth is, all the POWs round here often work alone. There aren't enough guards to go around. And now that they've separated the hardcore Nazis and opened a camp just for them, the rest of these fellas pose no problem. There's nowhere for them to go, for one thing. Cause no problem at all."

"I don't like it," Jimmy said.

Ed gave a light chuckle. "Last year it was Zach Wells who drove them to and from camp, and Otto carried around his old gun from the Great War. But it was never loaded. Decided it wasn't worth the effort of lugging it around. Otto likes farm work, and would rather be busy than twiddlin' his thumbs. No harm done."

"I just can't get over the fact that the enemy is here! On our farm! I traveled nearly ten thousand miles to get away from all that."

Ed took off his hat, and repositioned it on his head. "I understand how you feel, but look around you. How do you think we were able to keep the farm running? And at a profit. We were lucky to get these three. Hard workers, all of them. And they're not Nazis."

"They're scum. And I don't like all this friendliness. The last thing I expected to see at home was my mother and sisters all chatty with a bunch of Krauts. They're the enemy and it's best to keep that in mind."

*

The phone rang all morning for Jimmy. Word had gotten around that he was home, and when he and Ed returned for lunch, he spent a good half hour returning calls and making promises to meet his buddies in town that night.

Kate hovered over Jimmy at lunch, insisting that he have another slice of meatloaf and more stewed tomatoes.

Ursula scooted the bread and butter closer to him. "You don't have to skimp on the butter, Jimmy. That's something we have enough of. For now, at least."

"I'm not skimping, but all the corners are getting filled," he said. "Nothing beats a home-cooked meal."

Kate sat across from him, happy to see him enjoying her cooking. "I wish you'd leave the farm alone and just enjoy yourself, Jimmy."

"Don't you worry. I won't be missing any of the dances or parties. But me and Ed," he nodded to the old farmhand who sat across from him, "we got our work cut out for us, don't we?"

Ed leaned back in his chair, his thumbs hooked around the straps of his overalls. "Well, if you're hell-bent on whitewashing, then we'd better get to it soon. The Farmers' Almanac is predictin' a cold winter, with lots of snow."

"Whitewashing?" asked Kate. "That can wait. I want you to relax while you're home."

"I will. But that doesn't mean I can't get a few things done. I want to build that trellis and gate for you, Mom. And if I have time, I want to repair the granary and machine shed. We've got the manpower. But first I'm going to whitewash the barn. It's all dark and dingy inside."

"All that would take months, in addition to their regular work," said Kate, clearing his plate away.

Jimmy stretched out his legs. "You all say what hard workers they are. Let's put it to the test."

Ursula placed bowls of canned pears in front of him and Ed. "Remember, Jimmy, these men are paid laborers, not slaves." She squeezed his shoulder playfully.

"They're Nazi POWs. And they never had it so good. You think our prisoners are getting paid? Getting home-cooked meals? Are warm?"

"The barn does need cleaning," said Kate, eager to avoid an argument. "But everything else can wait." She smiled as Jimmy stifled another yawn. "Look at you. You barely slept. Why don't you rest a bit?"

"Go on, Jimmy," said Ed. "Do as your mother says. I'll go check on the others. It'll be good to get that timber cleared out."

"I didn't come home to sleep," he said with another yawn. "But maybe I'll just catch a few winks. I promised a few of the fellas I'd meet them in town tonight."

"You'll be in no shape for town in this state," said Kate. "Go on."

Jimmy walked heavily to the living room. "I'll just stretch out for a bit. If I fall asleep, make sure you wake me in ten minutes. Got a lot to do."

He dropped onto the couch and was soon asleep. Kate went in to look at him, and it was all she could do not to stroke his hair, his cheek. Her little boy. She knew if she stood there staring at him, she would start thinking about Eugene, and Francy, and the tears would begin to fall. She walked back to the kitchen and spoke in a soft voice to Ursula.

"He's exhausted. I wanted to wash his things, but that can wait. I don't want to wake him."

Ursula nodded. "Maybe now's a good time for me to get caught up on the ironing, while it's quiet."

"And I'll get started on dinner," said Kate.

She had earlier taken out the pot roast from the butcher's and set it in the sink. Now she ran down to the cellar to get vegetables for Jimmy's favorite meal. She used her apron to hold the potatoes, onions, and carrots. And apples. She would make him an apple pie. She lightly hummed to herself as she laid everything out on the kitchen counter. This was the closest to normal she had felt in a good long time. Christmas! With her son home safe. She even took out a tablecloth from the trunk in her bedroom. It wasn't every day a son came home from the war.

She handed it to Ursula. "Can you press it? I thought it would be nice to use."

Ursula took the tablecloth and added it to the basket, glad that her mother was so busy with Jimmy. She smiled to hear the soft humming coming from the kitchen. Jimmy's presence took their minds off the fate of Eugene. With each day that passed, Ursula feared that they would soon receive the dreaded telegram. She noticed that her mother rarely checked the mail any more. She used to enjoy the walk to the end of the lane. But no more. And Ursula noticed that, if at all possible, she avoided going into town. She couldn't face the concerned faces, the gentle comments: "Any news yet?" or, "I'm praying for your son," or, "We've all lost someone." Instead she stayed home. And waited.

Thank God Jimmy was home. They would have Christmas together, and he would make sure it was a happy one.

While Ursula waited for the iron to get hot, she placed her hands on her lower back. She draped the tablecloth over the ironing board. A light pressing should do it. She sprinkled it with water and began to iron out the creases. Best to keep busy. In a few months, everything would come crashing down on her. She would have to say something. Soon. Thank God, Jimmy would be gone by then and would be spared the pain. It was a miracle that her mother hadn't noticed. Ursula knew it was because her heart was filled with worry about Eugene.

Two hours later, just as Ursula was finally getting to the bottom of the basket, she heard a truck pull up.

"Ursula!" Kate called. "Come in the kitchen. Joe Madden's here." She looked Ursula over as she came into the kitchen, holding the tablecloth. "Why do you always wear those baggy clothes? You used to care more about your appearance. Why don't you go and change?"

"It's just Joe, Mom. He knows we're running a farm. I don't have time to primp and curl like Sue Ellen."

Kate's face lit up as Jimmy came from the living room, rubbing his hands through his hair.

"What's all the commotion?" He saw the time on the kitchen clock. "You were supposed to wake me! I gotta get busy – "

"You have a visitor. Everything else can wait. Look!" Kate said, gesturing to the window. "Go find Ed and bring him inside with you. He could do with a break."

Jimmy went to the window and pulled the curtain further aside. "Holy smokes! Is that Joe Madden?"

Kate was just taking the pie out of the oven, happy that she had something fresh to offer. The kitchen was warm from the baking, and smelled of apples and cinnamon. "Ursula, how about you slice up some pie for us all? I've got the coffee going. Then sit down. I know how tired ironing makes the legs."

Ursula was glad for the break, and reached for some plates out of the cupboard. Through the window she saw Jimmy walking out to meet Joe, and then the old friends were slapping each other on the back.

Soon the kitchen table was full and enlivened with laughter and conversation. The two friends caught up and made plans for some late-season duck hunting. Then the conversation shifted to the parties and dances scheduled for Christmas. Joe blushed when Jimmy teased him about Sue Ellen.

"'Bout time you got married and started a family."

"Sue Ellen's pushing for a June wedding. Says all her friends are getting married."

"Everyone's in a hurry to marry these days," said Ed. "Soldiers and civilians alike." He took a bite of his pie. "Even the prisoners are getting married."

Joe cocked his head at Ed, incredulous. "You're joking. Now, how's that possible?"

"There's something called marriage *in absentia*. The POWs marrying girls back home. Complete with celebrations on both sides." He gave a chuckle and rubbed his chin. "Just no shiverees."

"Doesn't sound like much fun," said Jimmy, not wanting to talk about the POWs.

Joe nodded his thanks as Kate poured more coffee for him. "Puts a different spin on what a wedding is, that's for sure," he said.

"Makes you ask, just what is a marriage, doesn't it?" asked Ed.

"A piece of paper," said Jimmy, adding milk to his coffee.

"Flowers and a veil, to hear Jessica talk about it," Kate added.

Ed turned to Ursula. "What do you say?"

Ursula had been silent but now spoke quietly. "Surely, love is all that matters."

A soft smile came to Kate's lips. "That's true when you're young. And love is important. Of course, it is. But I'd have to say, it's the vows, and what's behind them that really count. That's what'll get you through the tough times. Partnership, the determination to make something work – like what your father and I had during the drought, the hard times. The love was always there – but something else kicked in."

Ed rubbed his chin. "Have to say I agree with you there, Kate." He took another sip of coffee. "I know Opal would say the same thing."

Joe broke the silence that followed by leaning back and saying, "To hear Sue Ellen talk, you'd think it was all about the wedding buffet and what she's going to feed everyone."

"Well," Kate said with a laugh, "she's got a point. The social part kind of holds it all together. To have family and friends with you at such an important moment in your life."

"I told Sue Ellen maybe we should wait until after the war. Otherwise she'll be serving up her rationing recipes. We'd have a chocolate potato wedding cake, along with some carrot pudding." He gave a shake of his head at the merit of some of her creations.

"Come now, I bet they were delicious," said Kate. "It's impossible for Sue Ellen to make anything that isn't."

Joe nodded at his future bride's reputation for being a fine cook. Then he grinned and took another bite of pie. "When I tell her how good this apple pie is, she'll fret all day, and tomorrow you can be sure she'll bake something special."

"You're a lucky man, Joe," said Kate. "Not everyone has her touch."

"'Deed I am."

The conversation shifted to the Corn-for-War show, with Joe and Ed telling Jimmy that besides the corn itself, the cobs were now being utilized.

"They mill them till they look like popped corn," explained Ed. "Treat 'em with some kind of acid and turn them into rubber and other products."

"We'll be planting most of our fields in corn this year," added Joe. There followed a debate between Kate and Ed about how much corn to plant in the spring.

Joe drained his cup. "I best be going. If I'm meeting you in town, I better stop by Sue Ellen's now or I'll never hear the end of it." He nodded his thanks to Kate and Ursula and slipped on his jacket.

Kate jumped up and ducked into the pantry. "Then you can drop off the walnuts I promised her – for her fudge."

Jimmy walked outside with Joe, followed by Kate. She handed Joe the bag of nuts. "Tell her I have more if she needs them."

Jimmy winced as he saw the difficulty Joe had going down the steps. The Guadalcanal hero having trouble with the porch stairs. "That leg giving you pain?"

"Nah. It acts up when I sit for too long. Gets a little stiff, is all. So that means we can't stay in one place too long tonight. We'll have to make the rounds."

Jimmy smiled in agreement. "I'll make sure we do. See you in a couple hours, Joe." He headed back towards the house and then turned to add: "I'll swing by and pick up Logan. I got a letter saying he'd be home on leave. Did you hear? The son of a gun made it through the Battle of Aachen without a scratch! They don't call him Lucky Logan for nothin'."

Joe had opened the door to the truck and was about to climb in. But he stopped. And didn't turn around or reply. He waited a moment, then lifted his face to Jimmy, then to Kate, who gave a small nod. Then he swung himself into the truck and drove off.

Jimmy noticed the exchange. "What? What was all that about?"

Kate swallowed. She had avoided telling Jimmy that his best boyhood friend had been killed. Now she wished she had told him.

Jimmy put a hand on the railing by the steps and looked up to the porch. "Mom?"

She watched the pickup truck drive down the lane, then lowered her eyes to Jimmy. "I'm sorry, Jimmy. I should have told you earlier. Logan – they say he caught a bullet as they were returning to base." Her heart broke at the pain that filled his face. She turned, and walked back inside, before her own pain began to show.

He gripped the railing. "God damn it," he said softly. Then he kicked at the dirt. "God damn it! This goddamn war!"

Ursula had stepped out on the porch to wave goodbye to Joe and heard what had passed. Jimmy raised his head at the voices coming from the farmyard and Ursula followed his gaze. Ed was heading over to Otto and the POWs who were just returning from the bottoms, the cart full of cut timber. Karl and Gustav were singing a song in German. Friedrich walked behind them, lost in his thoughts.

Ursula saw the change in Jimmy's face – his jaw clenched, his eyes narrowed. He muttered something under his breath, and began walking towards the group.

Ursula ran down the porch steps and hurried to catch up to him. "Look, here comes Jessica." She waved at her sister who had gotten off the bus and was walking briskly up the lane.

"Miss me?" Jessica cried, running up to Jimmy. Then she noticed his expression. She looked from Ursula to Jimmy. "We passed Joe. Did he stop by?"

Jimmy nodded, but kept his eyes on the POWs. His mouth twisted in disgust.

"What?" asked Jessica.

"Just found out that Logan was killed. By the stinkin' Jerries." He pointed with his chin to Friedrich. "Is that one always so goddamned moody? How can you stand to have him around?"

Friedrich looked up and met Jimmy's antagonism with a steely glare.

"Leave them alone, Jimmy," Ursula said softly. She took her brother's arm to go back into the house, but he shook it off.

Ed called out to Otto who was just driving the tractor into the farmyard. "Let's unload over here, against the shed."

Otto drove over to the shed, and waited for Gustav to unhitch the cart. Then they began to unload the tools and carry them into the shed. Friedrich followed last, taking the bucksaw and pruning saw.

Jimmy picked up a heavy coil of rope from the cart. "And this," he called out. He roughly threw it to Friedrich, catching him on the chin. Friedrich's eyes blazed with anger.

Jessica pulled on Jimmy's sleeve and said quietly, "Don't, Jimmy. He's sad. He's found out his family has been killed."

"Good!" Jimmy said, eyes on Friedrich. "The only good Kraut is a dead Kraut."

In a flash, Friedrich was on Jimmy, hurling him to the ground. Though it took Jimmy by surprise, he quickly broke free and defended himself. They were like two charging bulls in the dirt, lunging and heaving and rolling, using their elbows and knees to try to pin the other. They twisted to their feet only to land back on the ground in a tangle of rage, landing punches wherever they could. Both of them were tall and strong, and driven by hate.

Ed tried to get in between them. "That's enough, now!" But his wiry grip had no effect against the brute strength of the young men.

Ursula also tried to pull them apart, alarmed at the blood that ran from their noses and mouths.

But they were blind to anything other than their fury. They stumbled to their feet and fell against the side of the barn, throwing lightning punches that landed with thuds. Friedrich soon had Jimmy pinned against the barn with one hand around his neck.

"Friedrich!" Ursula cried. "Jimmy! Stop it! For God's sake, stop it!"

The two men eyed each other in hatred – then Friedrich's posture slumped. He dropped his hands and staggered backwards. Then he walked away, his chest heaving, and wiping the blood and sweat from his face.

Otto and the others came out of the shed on hearing the raised voices, and crossed over to the barn. They looked at Jimmy, who had his hands on the fence, coughing and trying to catch his breath, and then over to Friedrich, who was walking towards the pasture. Ed motioned for Otto to take Gustav and Karl back to the shed; the less said about what just happened, the better.

Jessica was shaking, angry at both Friedrich and Jimmy. "He shouldn't have hit you. But that was a mean thing to say, Jimmy. You shouldn't have – "

Jimmy lurched around and threw his arms out. "What the hell's wrong with everyone! Have you all lost your minds? He's a goddamn German soldier!"

Jessica gasped at the blood on his cheek, and covered her mouth. "Oh, Jimmy." Tears shot to her eyes and she started to go to him but he pushed her away.

"I'm going to report this." He stormed off towards the house, then whipped around with his finger jabbing the air. "And he's not coming back to this farm!"

Jessica followed him to the house. "Jimmy, wait! You're bleeding."

Ursula started to go after Friedrich but Ed grabbed her arm. "Leave him be." They watched him walk across the pasture, and go down to the creek. "That boy's in a world of hurt. Got so much sorrow in him he's about to burst."

Ursula twisted her arm to leave. But Ed tightened his grip.

"Ursula! It's not my place to say anything, but – "

His words caused her to remain rooted to the ground.

Ed squinted out to the pasture, not wanting to speak. Then he let go of her arm, and spoke gently. "Look. I know there's a sort of understanding between you two. I saw it long ago."

Ursula's breath caught in surprise and she started to speak.

Ed held his hand up. "I don't object. He's a good man."

Ursula's widened eyes confirmed what Ed had suspected. "But you understand that it can come to nothing. A friendship is one thing. You're level-headed enough to know that it ends there."

Ursula turned her face away, afraid of what it might reveal.

But Ed wasn't finished. "Don't go provoking your brother any further. Lord knows what he's been through. He needs this time at home to be peaceful."

She began to walk away.

"Ursula!" Ed added in a low voice. "Make sure Jimmy doesn't tell Otto what happened. He'll have to report it, and we don't want that."

Ursula was torn between which way to go. She looked at the house and could hear yelling from Jimmy, then over to the pasture.

Ed saw that her mouth was trembling. "I'll go talk to Friedrich. Though there's not much I can say. You go on inside. Go on."

She watched Ed cross the farmyard and open the pasture gate. Then she walked to the house.

Inside the kitchen, the aroma from the pot roast filled the kitchen. The table was beautifully set with the tablecloth. And there was Jimmy, pacing around the kitchen, ranting about the prisoners.

Kate grabbed a cloth and ran it under the faucet. She tried to dab at his cheek, but he kept pushing her hand away.

Jessica stood next to him, wringing her hands. "I'm sorry, Jimmy," she said. "I shouldn't have said anything."

Jimmy grabbed the cloth and threw it into the sink. "What's wrong with you all? Treating them like friends! And that bastard," he said, pointing to the farmyard. "I want him off the farm!"

"Lower your voice," said Kate. "We're not going to argue about this, Jimmy. I understand how you feel. And I'll make sure they stay out of your way from now on. But we need their help." She went to the stove, shut off the burners, and placed lids on the pans – trying to keep her calm. "For God's sake, try to imagine how you'd feel if you lost all of us. He has no one. His entire family has been killed."

"I can't believe this is what I came home to! A bunch of Nazi sympathizers! Good God, what would Francy say? And Eugene? Have you thought of what – "

Kate spun around, her eyes ablaze. "Don't you dare use my sons against me! I'm holding this farm together for you! For all of you!"

Jimmy's face burst into outrage. "I've been shot at! Had a ship sunk under my feet – twice! Been dived at by kamikazes!" He held his head in his hand. "And now it's followed me home! I can't get away from it!" He kicked at the chair and grabbed his jacket. "I've had enough of this." He left and slammed the door behind him.

"Jimmy!" cried Kate, following him to the door. "Jimmy, wait!"

Jessica and Ursula watched him through the window. He thrust his hands into his pockets and cut through the farmyard. Then he began to cross the fields of corn stubble, opposite the pasture.

Jessica spoke gently. "He's going to the Wulrich farm. Probably going to catch a ride into town with Burly. Don't worry, Mom. He just had to get it out of his system. It was building inside him since he got here."

Kate moved to the window, her arms tight around herself. Her shoulders shook as she watched him cut across the fields. "Home for two days – and this had to happen! Am I wrong? I have to keep the farm together. Doesn't he understand that? I have to! They're coming back. My sons are coming back."

Ursula knew how carefully her mother had planned the meal, how happy it made her to cook for Jimmy. Kate so rarely cried, but now tears were running down her cheeks. Before the death of Francy, Ursula had rarely seen her mother cry. Since then, there had been many times. Was she slowly breaking down? Ursula gently placed her hand on her mother's shoulder.

"He's always like this, Mom," said Jessica. "Quick to blow. He'll get over it." She exchanged a look with Ursula, and kept chattering, filling the air. "Don't worry. The guys'll get him out of his mood and …"

Ursula took a basket from the back porch and went outside to gather eggs. She didn't trust herself to speak. How could the world be filled with such misery? She couldn't bear it if Friedrich were taken away. Everything was going from bad to worse. She went to the back of the coop and leaned against it, stifling her tears. She stood there waiting in the darkening day, lifting her coat sleeve to her eyes. Soon she heard Otto's truck start, the door squeak open and slam, and then drive away with the POWs.

She watched as the sky slowly deepened from gray to ashy charcoal. Jimmy's words cut her to the core: "I can't get away from it." He had been in the heart of the war for over two years and must be sick of it. It *was* wrong that the enemy was here on his farm, while he was being shot at. And Paul so far away. And Eugene... She understood how Jimmy felt. But it didn't help.

*

Dinner was largely eaten in silence, with Jimmy's absence acutely felt. Ursula's heart was breaking for her mother. And for Jessica. This should have been a happy time for them. She and Jessica did their best to keep a conversation going about the Red Cross Christmas packages and Jessica's student teaching. But their words seemed to echo back into emptiness.

The evening hours passed slowly. They sat in the living room while they listened to the radio. Kate and Ursula mended clothes; Jessica did her homework. When the program came to an end, Jessica shut her book and said she was going to wash up and then work on her embroidery in her room.

"Are you going to wait up, Mom?" Ursula asked.

Kate nodded, but kept her eye on her sewing. "He'll be home soon."

Ursula went upstairs to take a bath, and then tried to read in bed. But it was useless. There was no way she could sleep until Jimmy returned. She knew her mother would be sick with worry until he was home and a few kind words could be spoken.

She got out of bed and knocked on Jessica's door and stepped inside. Jessica had set aside the quilt and was working on something lacey.

"How pretty!" Ursula said, holding up one side of the ivory netting; it was embroidered with tiny pink and ivory rosettes. "What's it going to be?"

Jessica tilted her head and studied her work. "I'm not sure yet. It's a new stitch I've been working on. Maybe a covering for a summer dress. What do you think?"

"It's lovely," Ursula said, holding it closer. "So delicate." She set it down, and then unfolded the quilt that was nearly finished. She looked at the quilting she had worked on over the summer, and then examined Jessica's embroidered depiction of their farm. "Your work is beautiful, Jessica. I'm sure this will make Mom happy."

Jessica looked up at the rare compliment and a look of concern crossed her face. "Ursula, I've – "

Ursula held up her hand and they stopped to listen. They went to the window and parted the curtain. A pickup truck drove up the lane and then up to the house. A truck door opened and closed with a bang, followed by some loud laughing and a horn tooting. Jimmy soon came into the house, singing.

"At least he's home," said Jessica. They crept into the hall to listen.

Kate had also heard the noise and set her sewing down. She went into the kitchen and saw Jimmy pull out a chair at the table and sit heavily on it.

"Evenin', Mom!"

"Evening? It's almost midnight." She stood next to him. "Did you have a good time?"

"Sure did. Got a ride home from Burly. We ran into Kyle and Petey Kroger."

"Did you have dinner?"

Jimmy pinched his eyebrows together as he tried to remember. "Lots of liquids, but no solids as I recall."

"I thought as much." Kate grabbed a dish towel and opened the oven door. Then she took out the plate of food she had kept warm for him.

Kate listened in silence as Jimmy ate his dinner and rambled on about the old friends he had seen, and news from town. Then he held out his hands, as if in the middle of an explanation. "Look, I'm sorry. I don't want to make anything worse. I want to make everyone happy. I got a temper. I always have."

He took a few more bites of food, but he was focused on the table. "I thought about it. What you said. If I lost all of you." His eyes filled at the tragic vision. "God damn! It was hard enough losing Francy. And I can't even think about Eugene. If

I lost everyone, all of you, I'd go crazy! I'd lose my mind. Course I would." He thought about it for a moment, a piece of buttered bread in his hand. "The only difference is, I woulda killed the son of a bitch who said anything about my family." He tore angrily into the bread.

Kate placed her hand on his shoulder. "Eat your meal and don't think of such things. And I don't like you drinking so much."

"Blame it on the Victory Quart, Mom. Bigger bottles – to save on metal caps!" He guffawed loudly at the idea. "We started drinking at Burly's before we went into town."

"It's not good for you." Kate sat down next to him again and examined his cheek.

"I gotta live while I can, Mom."

"Don't talk like that."

He took a few more bites. "I promise. I promise! Good behavior the rest of my time here. I came to make you all happy. That's all I want to do. I can kill Jerries and Japs when I go back. While I'm here, I just want to feel like I'm at home. Like the war was something that happened a long time ago."

He looked around as if suddenly realizing that Ursula and Jessica were not at the table. "Where's my soft-hearted sisters? Ursula! Jessica!" he hollered. "Come visit with your pig-headed brother!"

Jessica went down the steps, followed by Ursula, and stopped on seeing Jimmy. "You're a sight!"

Ursula stood in the doorway to the kitchen. There was Jimmy, slouched at the table, his cheek purple where Friedrich had punched him. Her stomach clenched and she went to him. "Oh, Jimmy! Let me get some iodine for that."

He brushed her hand away. "Battle wound. Nothing more. God damn Nazi! Strong sucker. Took me by surprise." He pushed his plate away and Ursula brought it to the sink.

Jessica was eager to hear about his evening in town and was soon laughing at his stories.

Ursula spoke softly to Kate, who appeared worn out. "I'll clean up, Mom."

Kate nodded. "I'm going to bed." She placed a hand on Jimmy's shoulder, but addressed Ursula. "Don't let him stay up late. He needs his rest." Kate kissed his forehead and left the room.

Ursula washed the dishes while Jimmy and Jessica talked.

But after a while, Jimmy leaned his head on his hand, and closed his eyes.

"I'm going to bed," said Jessica. "I have school tomorrow. Night, Jimmy."

Jimmy stumbled into the living room. "Whoa! Feels like I'm back on ship." He held his arms out to the side while the room righted itself. Then he fell heavily onto the couch, and stretched out with a loud groan. "Just gonna rest a bit."

Ursula followed him in. "Don't do that, Jimmy. You'll fall asleep. You'll sleep better in bed. Come on." She tugged on his arm but he didn't budge.

"Just twenty winks." He shifted his weight around trying to get comfortable, and she saw him wince, as if in pain.

"Did – did he hurt you?"

"Who?" He looked at her in genuine confusion. "Oh, the German?" He gave a slight smile. "He coulda hurt me a lot worse, let me tell you. The sucker went easy on me."

"I'm sorry that had to happen, Jimmy." She handed him the pillow from the armchair.

He waved away her words. "For two years, I've been ready to fight. Just waitin'. All pumped up." He made fists, and threw a few punches into the air. "Then, all of a sudden – I'm home. On the farm. I gotta remind myself I'm not in the Pacific. It's all corn fields now. Soy beans." He chuckled lightly and positioned the pillow beneath his head.

Ursula sat on the chair next to the couch and observed him. A soft light from the lamp fell on his face. "What's it like? At war. On ship."

"Boring," he answered with his eyes closed.

"I'm serious. Other than the news reels, I have no idea what it's like. Sometimes I try to imagine what you and Paul – and Eugene – are doing and seeing, and I can't come up with an image. Your letters never give any clues. You all say that everything is fine and that you miss home and want letters. But you never say anything about the war."

"Because we can't. All our mail is censored, you know that. Besides, no one wants to talk about it. And I don't think anyone really wants to hear about it."

"I do," said Ursula.

He cocked his head to her. "Why?"

Ursula shrugged. "I want to know what happens. What it's really like."

"It's a goddam war, Ursula. What do you think happens? We shoot and get shot at. That's about it." He readjusted the pillow, trying to get comfortable.

"Most of the time we're bored out of our minds, playing stupid games to pass the time, reading comic books. Then, all of a sudden we're called to action. And the horror begins. Dive bombed from the sky. Torpedoed from the water. Sometimes you feel like you're surrounded and don't stand a chance."

Jimmy closed his eyes again, as if he had said all he wanted to. But Ursula pushed on. "Have you – have you seen the enemy?"

Jimmy opened his eyes and faced her. "You mean have I killed the enemy?"

Ursula didn't know what she meant. She wasn't sure how much she really wanted to know.

"Of course, I've seen the enemy. What the hell do you think I'm out there for? It's kill or be killed."

She waited for him to say more.

"Why do you think I'm home? My first furlough in two years." He pulled up his shirt and revealed a burn mark on his side, scarred and red.

Ursula covered her mouth and knelt beside the couch. "You're hurt? Oh, Jimmy, are you all right?"

"All right enough to be going back. But our ship is in repairs. Lucky break for me, or I wouldn't be here now."

"Are you in pain?"

"Now and then. This is nothing compared to other – " he didn't finish his sentence, but she saw a slight twitch at his mouth.

"What – what happened?"

"We took a hit. I was thrown into water covered with burning oil. They fished me out. Minor burns, is how they described what I got. Trust me, I was one of the lucky ones. There were guys on ship – we couldn't decide if there was enough left to bury or not."

She suddenly remembered his reaction earlier in the day to the package from the butcher. It was open in the sink, bloody. Jimmy had come up to her and when he saw it, he stopped, stared at it, and quietly left the room.

"One kamikaze got so close I saw his goddam face! We shot him down." He briefly faced her. "They're crazy, you know that? We came across a raft of Japs a few days after we sunk their ship." He stared out into the room, seeing the vision once again. "We went to pull them out. But they believe there's shame in being taken prisoner. So, one of them – an officer I guess – shot them. One by one. Put a pistol in their mouths." He imitated the act. "Only one of them fought. But the others held him down. Then waited their turns. Then he turned it on himself. A lot of blood. Made the sharks happy." He closed his eyes again and rested his hands on his chest.

Ursula's eyed widened in horror, but Jimmy continued to narrate the scenes in his head. Now and then he would open his eyes and squint at the ceiling, as if to confirm a detail.

"And our guys? I've seen faces blown off, men screaming in agony. And we're on ship. The infantry has it even worse. The Marines? Jesus Christ! The things we hear. The hand-to-hand combat on those God-forsaken islands. Banzai attacks. Better off dead than captured by the Japs."

He was quiet a moment, then gave a wry laugh. "Even if you survive, there's the other stuff that'll get you. Dengue fever. They say it won't kill you but you wish it would. Malaria. Jungle rot. One of my buddies has a brother in Borneo – lost his testicles to jungle rot. Now what do you think his fiancée is going to say about – " he stopped midsentence, suddenly aware of what he was saying.

He looked over at Ursula. Her cheeks were streaked with tears, but she was silent.

He put his head in his hands. "What am I saying? Jesus Christ, I'm sorry, Ursula. Don't listen to me. Don't ask me anything more. There's just a pile of garbage in my head and sometimes I can't stop it coming out."

He rubbed his hands through his hair. "I don't know what I'm saying. Everything is just so messed up. I can't stop thinking about Eugene. My big brother. If anything happens to him…" Tears welled up in his eyes, and he roughly brushed them away.

"Look, forget everything I said. Don't you dare tell Mom any of this. Not Mom or Jessica, you hear me?" He waited for her to promise.

"I won't."

"And you forget what I said."

"I'm sorry, Jimmy. I'm so sorry."

"What the hell are you sorry about? It's war."

After a few moments, he let out a burst of hilarity. "Ole Petey got shit faced and walked into the wall! Had us howling. Then – then he started arguing with the wall, threatening it!" His words were garbled up in his laughter.

Ursula gave him a smile, as if a door had been mutually closed. A door that had opened onto hell. "Why don't you go upstairs to bed?" Ursula gently coaxed him.

"I will. In just a minute." Jimmy had closed his eyes. "Twenty winks is all I need."

For a moment, Ursula thought he had fallen asleep. But then his face scrunched up and she wondered if he was in pain.

"You know, I keep thinking about that Jap in the raft who fought back. I keep thinking that he must've had someone he wanted to see again. A son, a wife, his mother. To hell with ancestral honor. He wanted to see his home again." He rolled on his side, wincing. "Jesus Christ! I can't believe they got Logan. Lucky Logan. Goddamn war."

Ursula sat with him for several minutes, until she heard his breathing deepen. Then she took the quilt that was folded on the armchair and covered him with it, and switched off the lamp.

She stood a few moments in the dark, only a faint light coming from the kitchen. She wished he didn't have to go back. She wanted him home where he was safe, where they could look after him. Those poor, poor boys, she thought. So far from home. Part of such horror. Even in the dim lighting she could make out the bruise on his face. The bruise that Friedrich, the enemy – her lover – had given to him. She buried her face in her hands.

Chapter 7

❧

Lillian had agreed to meet Izzy for lunch at their old place, and couldn't wait to tell her the news – Charles had called from Virginia! He was on U.S. soil, safe! And he would arrive home next week. She had been distracted all day just thinking about it.

She felt Izzy's absence acutely. Just know ing that her friend and ally was close at hand had been a source of comfort and support during her years at Rockwell Publishing. She had met other women over the years and was on a friendly basis with several of her colleagues. But there was no one like Izzy.

Lillian had passed Mr. Rockwell once or twice since Izzy's departure, and he had glared at her, as if it was her fault that Izzy left. Lillian knew that he truly missed Izzy, and was probably hurt by her departure. But he could be impossible. Dicta-torial, brash, demanding. Lillian had experienced her own ups and down with him. But fight it as she might, she had a soft spot for Rockwell. She had the impression that he just couldn't help himself.

And she thought he must be lonely. Divorced four years ago, he flitted from affair to affair, but he never seemed happy.

The rumors had floated up to her that things were falling apart in the main office. Izzy's absence showed Rockwell just how important she was.

But it was too late; Izzy had made up her mind. Lillian hoped there was a chance that she might come back, if only because she knew how much Izzy loved her job. She had really blossomed over the years, rising from typist to office manager, to Rockwell's right-hand "man." But Izzy rarely changed her mind about anything.

Lillian hurried out the office and soon the two friends were sitting together at the coffee shop, Lillian full of her news from Charles.

"Izzy, I can't tell you how happy I am. It's all I can do not to jump on the train and wait for him down in Virginia." She answered Izzy's arched eyebrow. "Yes, I already suggested it. But he has to travel to Washington, and then go back to Virginia for a few days. But after that, we'll have three weeks together."

"I'm happy for you, Lilly. The boys must be beside themselves."

"They are. And they're so excited that he'll be here for their play. They're taking it so seriously. They're at Mrs. Kuntzman's tonight, interviewing her. Charles will be surprised at how much they've grown since the spring. Oh, Izzy, I can hardly wait."

"And when do you meet with that art director? I'm dying to know what she has to say."

"Me too! On Wednesday. Even if nothing comes of it, it's gotten me back on the path I want to be on – doing freelance work. I told Charles about the meeting. He's been encouraging me to work independently for years. I didn't feel ready before, but I do now. I've learned so much at the publishing house. I really am grateful to Mr. Rockwell for taking a chance on me."

"He only did it because he needed you. Trust me, I know the man. He saw your work and saw dollar signs. But still, I'm glad it worked out as it did." Izzy took a sip of coffee, and then turned the cup around on the saucer, her mouth twisted in thought. "Has he said anything?"

"You mean Mr. Rockwell? No. But there are rumors that things are not going very smoothly with you gone."

"That's nice to hear," Izzy said with a cheerful smile. "Serves him right."

Lillian leaned forward on her elbows. "But tell me all about life in the shipyard! I still can't believe you're training to be a welder."

"*Was* training."

Lillian sat up and blinked in surprise.

"I quit. Gosh, I hope this isn't becoming a pattern with me." Izzy gave it a quick thought, shrugged, and took a bite of her sandwich.

"What happened? Didn't you like it?"

"I'm not cut out for that kind of work. The men don't like us being there, and they let us know. We get paid less for doing the same job they do, which really irks me. The work is monotonous, as far as I can see. But to tell the truth, Lilly, it's those coveralls! And wrapping my hair in a turban. I don't want to sound shallow, but I can't see myself dressed like that for the duration, as they say."

"I can't say I blame you," said Lillian. "Wearing something pretty helps to make the day more enjoyable. When everything else is going wrong, a nice dress or a pretty sweater seems to help. So, what will you do?"

"I've found another office job. Gasoline fraud rationing. The black market, racketeering. Gas chiseling. We'll see. It doesn't sound too exciting, but at least I can wear a dress." She took another bite of her sandwich. "I don't see it as long-term. Gas rationing is slowly easing up now that our pipelines have been built."

"And then what will you do?"

"Who knows? But I'm not worried. I'm a saver and I've invested. By the time my war bonds mature I'll be set. Assuming we win this war."

"Of course, we'll win. They say the war in Europe will be over soon. The Allies are pushing towards the Rhine. It won't be long now."

Izzy gazed out the window. "I hope so. But how they'll ever get through the Siegfried Line is beyond me."

*

Mrs. Kuntzman opened her door to the young playwrights, and they were greeted by her smiling face, her flour-dusted green apron, and a warm waft of cinnamon and apples.

"Come in, come in! I have apple strudel for youse all, fresh from the oven!"

She stopped short when she saw Henry, and tucked her chin in surprise.

"This is my friend I told you about. Henry," said Gabriel. "This is Mrs. Kuntzman, our babysitter, and one of the best cooks in the whole wide world."

Mrs. Kuntzman clasped her hands. "*Mein Gott im Himmel*! I expected a little boy. Come in, come in."

Henry offered his hand. "Henry Hankel, at your service, ma'am." He inhaled deeply through his nose, turning his head side to side. "If I'm not mistaken, that's genuine Bavarian *apfelstrudel*, just like my *Oma* used to make. Ten to one there're raisins in there."

"*Ach*! Sadly, there are no raisins to be found, but otherwise is genuine." Her eyes twinkled with delight. "So, you know German baking? Then you will be my official taster. Say if as good as your Oma's."

"That's going back quite a long time. But I'm honored by the appointment."

Tommy and Amy exchanged a glance at the immediate rapport between the two older people. Then they all headed straight for the kitchen, with Gabriel and Billy leading the group.

Mrs. Kuntzman held up a finger, with Henry walking by her side. "The secret is in the dough. You must roll and pull it," she said, imitating the action, "until it is paper thin."

"Thin enough to read a newspaper through it," Henry confirmed.

"Ah, you know the test. So, your Oma was a true baker!"

"All I know is that it tasted like heaven."

"How about coffee for you, Mr. Hankel?" She placed a hand on Gabriel's shoulder. "And mint tea for the children?"

Soon they were all sitting around her kitchen table. While they enjoyed the warm strudel and their tea and coffee, Amy gave a synopsis of the play and described the characters.

A shadow crossed the old woman's face. "The Great War. A terrible time. Terrible." She said something in German under her breath.

Tommy looked at the others and then turned to his old babysitter. "Mrs. Kuntzman, it's all right if you don't want to talk about it. We could ask you questions about something else from that time."

Gabriel leaned into Henry and whispered. "Her only son was killed in that war."

"No, no." Mrs. Kuntzman waved away any sad memory, and smiled. "You come for interview, and I will give interview. You, too, were there, Mr. Hankel?"

"Please. Henry. Indeed, I was. Mostly in France. Cambrai in '17. Wounded at Meuse-Argonne in '18. Sent home. But this here play takes place in Flanders, if I'm not mistaken?"

Tommy nodded and described the location, the stage sets, and their costumes.

Mrs. Kuntzman showed intense curiosity about every detail and questioned all of them about their roles. When it was time to start taking notes, she began to clear the table.

Henry took his dishes to the sink.

"No, no, stop that! I take care of dishes," protested Mrs. Kuntzman, laughing and pulling him away from the sink.

Amy jumped up to help, nudging Tommy and Mickey, and they soon had the table cleared.

"Dishes can wait." Mrs. Kuntzman took off her apron and waved everyone away. "Now. All to living room for interviews."

Amy had a list of items to be discussed for both Mrs. Kuntzman and Henry, but soon the others joined in with their own questions: What food did they eat? How did they celebrate Christmas? How long did it take for letters to arrive back then?

Mrs. Kuntzman had placed an album on the coffee table, full of photos, newspaper clippings, and letters from her son, and referred to them now and then as she answered their questions and recounted stories.

Henry had details about the Spanish Flu epidemic that took so many lives, including his wife and infant son. He also provided details about foxholes and sea transportation, and had several humorous tales that set them all laughing.

When Mrs. Kuntzman brought out her son's medals, Gabriel had what he thought was a brilliant idea.

"Hey! How about we name our hero after your son? Would that be okay?"

Mrs. Kuntzman placed her hands on her chest, touched. "That would make me very happy."

Tommy positioned his pencil. "Good thinking, Gabe. What was his name?"

"Heinrich Leopold," she said with pride.

The faces dropped at the distinctly Teutonic-sounding name. Tommy's hand froze in mid-air.

Mrs. Kuntzman's eyes twinkled in mischief. "But he always went by Leo."

After another half hour of questions and reminiscing, the clock chimed.

"Ah, look at the time!" said Mrs. Kuntzman, jumping to her feet. "Two hours. Your mother will be worried."

"Nah," said Tommy. "She knows we're with you. But I guess we should be going."

When they made plans for the next session, Mrs. Kuntzman insisted that Henry join them.

"It's so nice to talk with someone who remembers the old days," she said. "And who appreciates my strudel!"

While they put on their coats and boots, Mrs. Kuntzman hurried to the kitchen to wrap a piece of strudel for Lillian, and a separate piece for Henry.

*

After several days on penicillin, Charles was much improved. His fever was almost gone, his appetite was increasing, and his energy was slowly coming back. The hallucinatory hodge-podge of images was gone, along with his disorientation and despair. He was able to read his letters with a much clearer head. His heart had swelled when he saw all the letters waiting for him on his arrival

– from Lillian, of course, but several from Tommy and Gabriel, unable to contain their excitement at seeing him again.

He carefully reread their letters, especially those from Gabriel. What had so disturbed him and made him dream that Lillian had left him for a younger man? He blamed it all on the fever and his weakened state.

He smiled through most of Gabriel's letter. Then a furrow slowly began to form between his eyes. There was that name again. Henry. Gabriel referred to him as his friend, but clearly he was older, a veteran. Charles couldn't help but wonder if he was also Lillian's friend. She must know him well if he volunteered at the hospital – they must work together there. Against his better judgment, he imaged a young, handsome veteran, helping with the boys, helping the wounded vets, helping Lillian. There were so many Dear John letters – the wait was hard, he knew…

He stopped his thoughts. Lillian was rock solid. He was absolutely sure of that. But maybe Henry… No. She would be in control of any situation, and was perceptive. She would make her feelings clear.

Charles lifted a pen and a sheet of paper. He would write her a brief letter. To let her know that he was much better and would be home soon.

But as he wrote, he thought of Gabriel's descriptions of the man. How they rode the bus home together. How Henry liked good cooking. How Lillian liked his company. What did that mean?

Gabriel referred to the man as older, which, to Gabriel, most likely meant thirty or forty. Perhaps this man had befriended the family. Lillian's soft heart was like an open door to anyone who came knocking. He imagined her with this younger man, Henry, helping out with the boys – perhaps bringing her some comfort in her loneliness? No. That was not her way.

And yet a heaviness pressed on his heart. He would see for himself. One week. What would he find? Whatever it was, he would deal with it. He held the pen, poised in the air. He would tell her, in not so many words, that…What? He hoped nothing had changed? He couldn't write that.

His mind felt all fuzzy again, but he finished writing his letter in time for the next mail pick up. Then, overcome with weariness, he sank into a deep sleep.

Chapter 8

❧

Ursula splashed cold water on her face to try to hide the lack of sleep, to minimize the shadows, the red eyes. All night her mind swam with terrible pictures: the things Jimmy had described; his burn wound; the image of Friedrich and Jimmy fighting – the sound of their fists hitting each other; the thought of Friedrich, his entire family gone. She felt sick to her stomach. She worried that Jimmy would force him to leave the farm. What would she do? What if he was transferred to another camp? Another state? She lay awake in knots, hour after hour, fretting about her predicament.

She went downstairs to find that her mother and sister were already outside taking care of the animals. She should have gotten up earlier, she thought, pulling on her jacket and walking out to the barn. She helped to feed and water the cows, taking a few moments to stroke her favorite, Clover.

Kate noticed the shadows under Ursula's eyes. "You look like you didn't sleep a wink. Did you and Jimmy stay up late talking?"

"A bit."

Jessica was milking one of the cows and eyed her sister from her milk stool. "By the looks of him last night, he won't be up any time soon."

"He will," said Ursula. "He'll want to get started on his projects."

Kate looked over at Ursula. "Why don't you go and start breakfast? Let's make him pancakes."

When Ursula hesitated, Kate urged her. "Go on, Ursula. We'll finish up here."

Ursula nodded and walked back to the house. In the east, low clouds along the horizon filled with color, and she walked to the edge of the porch to better see the sunrise. The delicacy of color, all lavender and apricot, tugged at her heart, and she felt a rush of tenderness for the beauty of the morning. The weeks were passing by; winter was settling in. A hard frost glistened on the bee-hives out by the fruit trees and on the brick side-walk that ran through the garden. The only color to be found now was in a few straggly marigolds; a hint of purple and old yellow in the browning chrysanthemums; the softest of pink in the faded roses that now hung their heads. Ursula hugged herself against the cold, and went inside.

She began to prepare breakfast, boiling water for coffee, and cutting up potatoes for home fries. Then she lifted down the large earthenware bowl, and set out the ingredients for pancakes. Kate and Jessica were soon at her side. Kate took over the mixing of the pancake batter, while Jessica began to make scrambled eggs and bacon. The kitchen filled with the smells of a farmhouse breakfast, under-pinned with the rich aroma of fresh coffee.

Kate straightened the silverware, and rear-ranged the jars of jam. She stopped and listened. "I hear him. Go ahead and get the pancakes started," she said to Ursula.

"And I'll start toasting the bread," said Jessica.

They heard the shower run, and fifteen min-utes later, Jimmy's footsteps sounded on the stairs.

Ursula heard Otto's truck pulling into the farmyard. She went to the window, hoping to catch a glimpse of Friedrich. Thank God, he was there. She had feared that he wouldn't come back.

"Does that ever smell good!" Jimmy came into the kitchen, draped his arm around Kate's shoulder, and kissed her cheek.

Kate touched his bruised face, but he brushed her hand away.

"My cheek's fine. But my head's all cottony. Guess the boys and I had a little too much fun last night."

"You were plastered, Jimmy," said Jessica.

"Yeah, well… Coffee'll help."

Jessica set the coffee pot on the table. "I hope you're hungry."

"You barely ate two bites for dinner," Kate said.

Jimmy looked around, trying to remember dinner. "That must be why I'm starving. Could eat a horse. Probably will before this war is over," he added.

He put his hands on the back of a chair and looked at all the dishes filling the table. "Look at that! And pancakes?" He smiled over at Kate. "That must mean you're not sore at me, right?"

"Maybe so, but I don't want you drinking so much – and on an empty stomach," she said, shaking her head at the thought.

"Okay, okay. It's gonna take me a while to get my sea legs, as they say. Dodging Japs one day, fighting Nazis here on the farm the next. Catching up with people I haven't seen in two years. Might take me a couple of days."

Kate looked over her shoulder at him and smiled. "Here. Take this to the table. And let's eat while it's hot."

He reached for the platter of pancakes and set it in the middle of the table. Then, hearing the voices from outside, he moved to the window.

Otto and the POWs had hitched the cart to the tractor. Ed spoke a few words to Otto, looked up at the sky, and then pointed to the pasture.

"Have a seat, Jimmy," Ursula said.

"Don't tell me they're here on the weekend!"

Jessica pulled him to the table. "Just Saturdays. We requested it and it's allowed."

Kate pulled out a chair and sat down. "We need all the help we can get. And they'd rather be earning script than doing nothing. They've been clearing out the trees down in the bottoms and need to finish up. We promised Mrs. England a cord of wood before the cold sets in." She glanced sideways, hoping that he would let it go.

Ursula put a spoon into one of the jars. "Look, Jimmy. Jessica set out her prize-winning honey and blackberry jam just for you. Make sure you praise them," she added with a smile.

"Second place for the jam," Jessica said, still disappointed that she didn't win the blue ribbon. "Even though it's a hundred times better than Sue Ellen's."

Jimmy laughed and sat down at the table. He poured himself a cup of coffee, added milk to it, and took a sip. He looked out over the table, at his mother and sisters.

"This is exactly what I miss most. Home-cooked meals, just sitting in the kitchen with you all."

Kate tried not to show it but her heart was brimming with joy that one of her sons was at the table. That she could cook for him, tend to him, protect him. She felt her eyes tearing up and jumped up to go to the pantry. "I think I still have some plum preserves in here somewhere," she called out.

Ursula heard the tremor in her mother's voice and exchanged a glance with Jessica. "There's plenty here, Mom. We can't spoil him."

"The guys on ship would be jealous as all get-out. Sit down, Mom." He took a helping of fried potatoes and two pancakes. Then he spread butter on the pancakes, poured maple syrup over them, and took a bite. "I forgot how good breakfast could be."

Ursula smiled at Jessica's happiness, which always showed in her lively chatter. She told Jimmy all about her school training, the dances coming up, and how everyone was saving their sugar coupons for the taffy pull at the Bloomfield's party. Then about how much she was earning from the eggs and milk.

"Good for you," said Jimmy. "Still selling at the market?"

"No, to Mr. Brook's store. That way I don't have to mess with taking ration coupons."

"Seeing it's Saturday, how about I take you girls into town to deliver the eggs and milk? You, too, Mom. We'll stop by – "

"Oh, you go in with the girls, Jimmy. I have a hundred things to get started on."

Jimmy was about to protest when he caught Ursula's glance and the tiny shake of her head.

"All right, Mom. Just give us a list of what you need. We'll pick it up."

"I'll stay and help you, Mom," said Ursula.

"Absolutely not! You go on with your brother. Have lunch in town. It would make me happy."

"Do you need anything from the dry goods store?" Jimmy asked.

"You could pick me up some batting – Jessica seems to have used it all. Oh, and some white thread."

"You don't fool me, Jimmy," said Jessica. "You just want to see if Gladys Wilkins is there."

Jimmy gave her a wink, but didn't say anything. Over breakfast he talked about how he wanted to spend his time on leave, and told stories about the sailors he met from different places. And he kept praising Jessica's honey and jam, making them all laugh.

Kate seemed to come to life, enjoying the playfulness of her children. She bustled about making sure everyone had what they needed, and insisted that Jimmy have another helping of everything. She wouldn't let the girls do any of the clean-up, and instead encouraged them to dress for town.

"And don't you dare think about wearing your coveralls. Put on something nice. It's not every day your brother comes home on leave."

"Don't worry, Mom," said Jessica. "But we have to wear our warm sweaters – it's cold out."

"Well, your nice ones, not those baggy ones you've been wearing," she called out after them as they went upstairs.

Ursula put on a skirt and a long blue cardigan over her blouse, and glanced at her reflection while she brushed her hair. Her amethyst earrings glittered as she moved her head from side to side. She lightly touched them. Her dream earrings, as she used to think of them. They were a gift from her family when she had been accepted to the women's college downstate, before the war. Jessica teased her that she never took them off. And it was true. She wanted a bit of dream-infused beauty close at hand.

She doubted now that she would ever go to college. Her world had shifted. And though she loved reading and learning, her dreams now were filled with Friedrich. All she wanted was to be with him, to live with him someday, as his wife. She brought her hand up to her earrings again, and her face softened in memory. How many times had Friedrich also touched them, claiming that he would one day buy her a ring to match.

Then she remembered the bruise on Jimmy's cheek and her smile vanished. And Friedrich was raw with pain and couldn't bear much more. The best remedy was to keep them apart. She had so wanted to speak to Friedrich, to comfort him – and to encourage him to avoid Jimmy. But she didn't want to attract attention to herself by asking again to stay home.

When she left the house, she saw that Ed was helping to load the milk canisters and eggs. Then he waved over at Otto and the prisoners who were returning from the bottoms with a load of timber. Otto drove the tractor over to the pile they had started a few days ago, and the prisoners were soon unloading the tree limbs.

"'Bout got 'er cleared," Otto hollered to Ed. "One more load should do it."

Ursula tried to catch Friedrich's eye, but he was avoiding her. Was he angry at her? Or was he just angry at life? She scanned his face and saw a bruise on his chin, a small cut under his nose; she had feared worse.

She saw Jimmy walk up to the group, and noted that while Gustav and Karl nodded their heads in greeting, Friedrich ignored him.

Jimmy turned his back on the POWs and faced Ed. "I'll pick up some lime in town, Ed. We can start the whitewashing on Monday."

Ed nodded. "Sounds good. We got another load to haul. Then the boys and I'll start prepping the barn. Sweep off the mud and cobwebs. Can you stop by the hardware store and pick up a new chain for the saw? Then the boys can get started on this," he said, stepping on a branch in the pile of timber.

"Why wait?" Jimmy jerked his head to Friedrich. "This one can get started." Jimmy took the axe that was leaning against the chopping stump and walked up to Friedrich. Friedrich met his gaze, but didn't reach for the axe. Jimmy tossed it to his feet.

Friedrich ignored him, and lifted another load from the cart.

Ursula pressed Jimmy's arm. "There's Jessica. Let's go."

Jessica ran down the porch stairs, her coat flying open. Ursula saw that she was wearing her new yellow calico dress and had tied a ribbon in her hair. Jessica checked on the eggs and milk, and then climbed into the cab of the truck and tooted the horn in impatience.

Jimmy turned to Ed and pointed his chin to Friedrich. "He's a surly bastard. Does he understand English?"

Ed ignored his comment. "And we could use a brush or two for the whitewash. We got a couple of brooms for the walls we can use."

Ursula threw Friedrich a look, to please let it go. For her sake.

He met her eyes briefly, then leaned down for the axe and walked to the pile of branches. He was soon swinging at the limbs, turning them into logs.

"Come on! We're late as it is," cried Jessica. She scooted to the middle of the seat and waved goodbye, giddy with excitement. She had dressed carefully, hoping that all her classmates would see her around town with her brother in the Navy.

Ursula climbed in next to her and closed the door, relieved when they were on their way. She leaned against the door and when they turned onto the country road, she gazed out the window at the barren fields, grateful for Jessica's chatter.

"Mom doesn't go into town much anymore," Jessica explained. "Not since the telegram about Eugene. She can't stand everyone asking if we've heard anything. So, she doesn't go. She doesn't even like to get the mail. Afraid of what she'll find there. So, I always get it on my way home from school."

"Can't blame her," said Jimmy. "Guess the home front has its own battles to fight. Never knowing. Waiting to hear."

"Did I tell you Shirley and I are in charge of the decorations for the Christmas dance? She asked me to pick up some paint for the banners we made. She's going to stop by tomorrow so we can start painting them. And we meet most nights after school, there's so much to do!"

Jimmy leaned forward and looked at Ursula. "What are you so quiet about?"

She gave a bright smile. "Just thinking about Christmas. And the presents I still have to make," she answered with a ready response. "Did you tell Jimmy what we're making for Mom?" she asked, knowing that Jessica would run with the idea.

"I'll show you when we get home, but you can't say a word." She then told Jimmy all about the quilt with the farmhouse picture and how it was almost finished.

After they had completed the sale of the eggs and milk, they bought what they needed from the hardware store, and then went into Arnold's Dry Goods. It was especially crowded, with women and girls choosing fabric for the upcoming holiday events and shopping for Christmas presents to be made. Green boughs tied with red ribbon framed the doorway and the scent of fresh pine greeted them on entering.

"Oh, look, Ursula!" cried Jessica. "Jimmy, will you help us cut some pine boughs? And get us a Christmas tree? It's not too early. See? Everyone else has already gotten started."

Mrs. Bloomfield and Shirley spotted them and immediately latched onto Jimmy, asking him question after question, and making him promise to come to their Christmas party. Jessica grabbed a shopping basket, and she and Shirley were soon pulled away by a friend from school who wanted their advice on which fabric to choose. Jimmy caught sight of Gladys Wilkins at the counter, whose face lit up when she saw him, and he was soon catching up with her.

Ursula began her shopping, smiling when she heard Jimmy ask Gladys if she had plans for the dance.

At the back of the store, she chose some thread and a set of buttons. Jessica handed her the basket, while she looked at ribbon and chatted with her friends. Ursula moved to the front counter to ask for the batting, and found that a commotion of sorts was going on. A newspaper was being passed around, to a mix of comments.

Mrs. Kryzinsky now had the newspaper and was waving it in the air, condemning the behavior reported in the article. Mrs. Bloomfield and a few others looked on skeptically. Ursula stepped closer to hear what the older Polish woman was so upset about. More bad news from her war-torn homeland, Ursula was sure.

Jimmy noticed Gladys's consternation at the raised voices and eased his way to the edge of the group. "What's all the uproar about?" he asked, giving a wink to Gladys. "Are they rationing something else now? Coffee prices going up again?"

Mrs. Bloomfield held her ground, arms crossed. "All I'm saying is that I don't believe it. You can't believe everything you read in the papers."

"Oh, it's true, all right," said Mr. Arnold. "Been hearing about it more and more. Now that there's so many of 'em here."

Jimmy raised his eyebrows to Mrs. Bloomfield to be let in on the information.

"German POWs – having American girl-friends," she said with a shake of her head.

Ursula stiffened and she felt herself grow pale.

Jimmy frowned at the idea. "Seems unlikely. They're in camps after all."

"Go ahead," said Mrs. Kryzinsky, shoving the newspaper into the hands of Mr. Arnold.

"Read it to one of *our* boys and let's hear what he has to say about it!"

The older man took the paper from her. "It's printed here in *Stars and Stripes*. A letter from Private First Class so-and-so. About a girl dumping her sweetheart for a German POW."

Jimmy cocked his head in skepticism.

Mr. Arnold looked over his glasses at Jimmy. "There's more. This fella's upset that the POWs go on excursions, and are visited by relatives – how they even had a sit-down strike. Prisoners!" He smacked the paper and scanned it for more disgraceful information. "Yes sirree. Says our boys are outraged that the POWs have sports teams, musical groups, and are earning college credit!" He finished up with a firm shake of his head and handed the paper to Jimmy.

One of the old-timers hooked his thumbs behind his suspenders. "Well, can't say as I blame 'em. Everyone wants to have a good time. It's human nature." He rubbed his chin and winced. "But our girls who go with these Germans?" He wagged his head in disgust.

Mrs. Bloomfield was not to be swayed. "I find it hard to believe. There might a few isolated incidents of foolish girls – "

"Foolish? Traitorous!" cried Mrs. Kryzinsky.

Jimmy glanced at the newspaper. "Most likely girls of German descent. Probably relatives or family friends." He tossed the paper onto the counter and leaned over to Gladys.

But the argument continued, and a young woman volunteered more information to fuel the fire. "My husband's uncle is a guard in Wisconsin and he says it happens a lot. That the fences around the camps are more to keep the girls out than the prisoners in."

Mrs. Bloomfield huffed. "Nonsense!"

"It does you credit to think so highly of our girls," said Mr. Arnold, "but this kind of thing goes on, I'm afraid. Look what happened to the women in France, cavorting with the Nazis. They cut off the hair of such girls, shaved their heads."

"Cut their hair? Their hair will grow back!" said Mrs. Kryzinsky, red with anger. "What kind of punishment is that? They should be shot!"

"A traitor is a traitor!" said another woman.

Ursula steadied herself against a wave of nausea, and made her way to the side door.

"Gladys," said Jimmy playfully, "you would never do such a thing, now would you?"

"Of course not!" she said, coloring.

"Especially with so many good-looking U.S. servicemen around," he said, taking her hand. A few people chuckled at Jimmy's remark and the group slowly broke up.

Gladys pulled her hand away, and tried to hide her smile as she rang up a customer.

Jimmy waited for her to finish, and then leaned in closer. "Can you join us for lunch at the Wood Duck?"

Gladys blushed a pretty pink. "I just had my lunch. Besides, I'm working."

"Aw, come on. Let me talk to Mr. Arnold. At least join us for a piece of pie or an ice cream soda."

She bit her lip and smiled. "All right. But I don't have my break until 2:00."

Jimmy's face burst into happiness at her answer. "We'll be waiting for you."

"Jimmy!" cried Jessica, running up to him. She held up a roll of blue satin ribbon. "For Mom's present," she whispered. "Isn't it pretty? Where's our basket?"

"Ursula had it. Let's get our things and go grab a bite. Gladys is going to join us for dessert. We can get the groceries afterwards."

They both looked around for Ursula.

"Now where'd she go?" asked Jimmy.

"I'll find her," said Jessica, leaving Jimmy to dally with Gladys.

Jessica looked down the aisles and at the back of the store, puzzled. Then she saw their basket by the side door and went outside. There was Ursula sitting on the bench on the side of the store. "What are you doing out here? I've been looking all over for you. Gladys is waiting to ring us up."

Ursula rose to her feet. "I just needed some air. It was so stuffy in there."

"Well, it's freezing out here. Come on. Let's finish up and have lunch. I'm starving, and the Wood Duck will be packed!"

*

Lunch took longer than expected, with Jimmy running into several friends and neighbors who all wanted to hear his stories and tell him their latest news. The owner insisted on treating Jimmy's table, and several people wanted to buy them desserts with war-themed names: the Flying Fortress Sundae, the Paratrooper Sundae that "goes down easy."

"That won't do," the owner protested. "Jimmy's in the Navy. I'll fix you up with something appropriate." He came up with a new concoction, a sort of banana split boat swimming in syrup. He shaped it with a whipped cream prow and when he stuck a tiny flag in it and presented it to Jimmy, cheers went all around. Jessica clapped her hands in delight, and Jimmy insisted that his sisters and Gladys help him with it.

Jimmy wouldn't let Gladys go back to work until she promised to see him again the next day. They decided on lunch at her house with her family, and then a movie. Ursula and Jessica exchanged glances, happy that Gladys so obviously adored Jimmy. She hadn't taken her eyes off him since she arrived.

It was late afternoon by the time they returned home. Friedrich was still splitting the wood, and most of the timber now lay in neat piles, the larger pieces stacked against the shed.

Jimmy jumped into the back of the truck and began handing the empty milk canisters to Ursula and Jessica to carry to the barn, while he and Ed brought the bags of lime.

Ursula noticed that one of the lunches inside the barn was untouched, and she knew immediately that it was Friedrich's. She glanced at Ed, but he turned and went back out to the truck.

"Boys about got all the cleaning done," said Otto, proud of the prisoners. "Finished the barn and started on the coop."

Jimmy had noticed the pile of wood and couldn't hide his surprise at Otto's announcement. The barn alone should have taken them all day, without the chopping of the wood.

"Told you they're hard workers," said Otto, returning to the truck with Jimmy and lifting out the rest of the supplies.

Jimmy winced at the sound of the wood being split. "Dang! I didn't say everything had to be done in one day. What's their hurry?" he asked, slamming the tail gate shut.

"That's the way they always work," said Jessica, also with a note of pride in her voice. She took the bags of empty egg cartons and headed towards the house.

Jimmy frowned. He gave Ursula the bag from the dry goods store, and he and Ed carried in the groceries.

Jessica told Kate all about town, the people they had seen, what they had bought, and how Jimmy had a date for tomorrow.

Ursula kept looking out the window, trying to hide the worry in her eyes. The air was filled with the rhythmic sound of the wood being split. She saw Gustav go up to Friedrich and speak to him, but Friedrich ignored his words, and kept swinging the axe. His jacket hung over the pump, and his shirt was dark with sweat.

Kate motioned to the sound of the chopping outside. "He hasn't stopped."

Jimmy spun around. "What do you mean, he hasn't stopped?"

Kate brought a few canned goods to the pantry. "Since you left. We've all tried to get him to take a break. Hasn't even stopped for lunch."

"Crazy dang Kraut!" said Jimmy. "What's he trying to prove?" He looked out the window.

Otto was now speaking to Friedrich, pointing to the darkening sky. But Friedrich just nodded and placed another piece of wood on the tree stump.

"He's going to hurt himself," said Jimmy, throwing his hands in the air. "Then he'll be no use to us. Maybe that's what he's up to."

Ed rubbed his chin. "He'll be sore all right. But he's never shied away from hard work. He's just taking up your challenge."

"He's being pig-headed," said Jimmy.

Ursula filled a glass of water and took it outside, determined to make Friedrich stop and eat lunch. She offered the glass to him, but he ignored it.

"Friedrich. Stop," she said in a low voice. "Your shirt is soaked. You'll catch a cold. Please, stop for now."

He stacked the wood he had just chopped, and placed another log on the stump, sweat pouring down his face.

"That's enough! Friedrich!" She wanted to scream at him, to jerk the axe away, to shake him to make him stop.

But he avoided her gaze, stopping only to stack up the wood.

Ursula went up to Ed, who had come out. "Can't you tell him to stop?"

"Been telling him all afternoon. We all have. He can be stubborn when he wants to be. Otto's the only one with any authority over him."

They overheard Otto, who was trying again to get through to Friedrich. "It's my head they're gonna have if I bring you back to camp in a mess." Ursula saw that Jimmy had come out and was coming down the steps, his face rigid with anger.

"Come on, Friedrich," said Ed gently. "That's enough, you can't – "

Just then Jimmy came and grabbed the axe from Friedrich. "Enough!" He threw the axe towards the barn.

He looked around the yard. Nearly all the trees had been chopped. Karl and Gustav had finished with the coop and were now stacking the remaining wood against the shed.

"That's enough!" cried Jimmy again. "Everyone just – stop!"

Otto motioned to the POWs. "It's going to be dark soon. Go wash up."

Ed pushed his hat back on his head, and stood next to Otto. "Good thing tomorrow's Sunday. He's gonna need the rest. Make sure he puts some ointment on that hand. It's sure to blister."

Otto drove over to the pump where the POWs were washing up, and waited for them to climb in. Gustav usually sat in front with Otto, but he tried to convince Friedrich to sit in the cab today.

Friedrich put his arm on Gustav's shoulder and said something in German. Then he climbed into the back of the truck, along with Karl.

Ursula threw a sharp glance at Jimmy, and returned to the house.

Jimmy stood with his arms crossed, watching the truck drive down the farm lane. When it turned onto the road, he kicked at the dirt and went inside.

Chapter 9

Lillian walked out of her meeting with Mrs. Huntington feeling that her life had just changed. And yet nothing was definite. Except that she now had an appointment with the director of children's books, to be commissioned for some illustrations! She could hardly believe it was happening. Seeds she had sown years ago had finally pushed through the earth and were feeling the warmth of the sun.

By the time their two-hour meeting had come to a close, all formalities had been dropped and the two women spoke of their children and husbands, where they had studied, and their ideas on art. Lillian hadn't had such a stimulating conversation about painting and creativity since her year in art school.

She could hardly wait for the next meeting. She arrived home full of hope for the future.

When she opened the door, she saw that Tommy and Gabriel were setting the table.

"I forgot to put the lasagna in when we got home, so it's only been in for about half an hour," said Tommy. "But I turned up the oven and it's kind of bubbling."

Lillian took off her hat and coat and gave them each a big hug. "Mmm, I can smell it. Let's take a look." She opened the over door and peeked inside. "Just right. Thank you, my darlings!"

"How was it, Mom?" asked Gabriel.

"Wonderful! We had such an interesting meeting." Lillian continued her conversation from the hallway and then the bedroom, raising her voice so they could hear her. As she changed out of her suit, she gave them the highlights, talking non-stop.

"Gosh, Mom, you're so happy," Tommy said when she returned to the kitchen. "Did you sell a lot of your stuff?"

Lillian smiled at his assumption and pulled out a few things from the refrigerator to make a salad. "Not yet. But it looks like I'll be commissioned to do some illustrations."

"Does she want you to work for her?" asked Gabriel.

"Well, this is just between us, but that is a possibility. We discussed it briefly. She has several women working part-time, and others freelancing. We're going to start working on a commission basis and see how it goes. Just think! I might be able to work part-time and be at home more."

"Just like Dad always wanted," said Tommy.

Lillian had to smile at the irony. She and Charles had quarreled many times over her job. He wanted her to quit and work on her drawings at home. And she was always dead set against it. She argued that she needed to keep learning in a professional environment in order to grow. But she felt that she had learned all she could at Rockwell's, and was ready to venture forth in a new direction.

"Yes, I think he'll be happy. I so rarely have exciting news about work. Won't he be surprised?" She set the salad on the table along with some bread sticks and they were soon enjoying dinner. Tommy and Gabriel talked over each other as they recounted their day and told her the latest updates on the Christmas program.

"Oh! Forgot to tell you!" Gabriel pushed back his chair and went to the table by the door. "Letters came from Dad – for all of us. We already read ours." He handed her an envelope and sat back down.

Lillian jumped up to take the letter and opened it in the living room, smiling as she read it. He wrote that he had had a fever, but was on the mend. A few meetings in Washington, D.C. and then back to Virginia for two days – and then he would be home. His words were full of such tenderness. But a sense of confusion suffused her at the cryptic sentiments he expressed at the end.

I understand your loneliness, and I can understand your wanting company. I certainly don't begrudge you that. I've always encouraged you to go out more.

Lillian looked up. What was he getting at? True, she had told him she missed him and was lonely. But she wrote that in nearly every letter.

I'm glad you have someone to help with the children, someone who can be there for you. Henry sounds like a wonderful man.

Lillian felt the blood rush to her face at the implication. Or was she imagining it?

"Gabriel," she said, returning to the table. "Have you been writing to your father about Henry?"

He shrugged. "Yeah."

"What did you say?"

He pinched his eyebrows in concentration. "I don't remember exactly. About how we help out in the rec room, and how I'm getting pretty good at ping pong. And about how me and Tommy are delivering posters with the Boy Scouts, and how Billy – "

"What did you tell him about Henry?"

"Just that he's our friend. And he's helping with the play. Why?"

"Did you mention his age or anything?"

"I don't think so. Dad wouldn't care about that."

She lifted the letter and read the lines again. And then burst out laughing.

"What, Mom?" Tommy asked

Gabriel looked from Tommy to Lillian. "What's so funny, Mom?"

"Sometimes your father can be very amusing." She left it at that.

*

After dinner Lillian sat down to write a letter to Charles. She would write a few nice things about

Henry, and say that she couldn't wait for them to meet. But she wouldn't say anything about his age.

She half listened to Tommy and Gabriel rehearsing their lines. She was familiar with most of the play, but Gabriel kept rewriting his lines, making Tommy nervous.

Gabriel was now standing in front of the couch, trying out his latest version of the prologue, with Tommy coaching him on his delivery.

Every now and then Lillian raised her head, catching a line or phrase that didn't seem to fit, or, rather, sounded vaguely familiar. She would listen for a few moments, then, not recognizing any more, resume her letter.

But the last line made her sit up.

"Gabriel!"

"You like it?" he asked, smiling.

"Well, yes. It's really coming along. Where did the lines come from?"

"All over the place," he answered.

"We all found stuff and then kind of pieced it together," explained Tommy. "Why? Does it sound bad?"

"Let me hear it again."

Gabriel began, but then stopped to add: "Remember, I'll be dressed in a costume like an old man. Kind of like Father Christmas, or Father Time. I haven't decided yet."

Lillian nodded and gave her full attention. Gabriel opened his arms in a dramatic welcome.

"Grrreetings family, grrrreetings friends!"

Tommy put up a hand. "Tone it down, Gabriel. We're not doing comedy."

Gabriel rolled his eyes, and began again in a more restrained manner.

"Welcome to all who have traversed from afar, over field and fountain, moor, and mountain."

Lillian opened her mouth, about to object to the lines from the Christmas carol, "We Three Kings."

"Our play tonight is about two soldiers, both alike in dignity, in awful Flanders, where we lay our scene. Cursed by an ancient grudge, and knee-deep in mud, they're surrounded by trenches and barbed wire and bullets – "

"Wait a minute," said Lillian. "Isn't part of that from Shakespeare? You can't use his lines like that. And it's about one soldier, isn't it?"

Tommy cracked his knuckles. "We were going to expand my role as his commanding officer. Maybe we'll have to forget that part."

Gabriel waited to see if there were more objections, then continued, reverting to melodrama.

"In a world of gathering gloom. Sorrow, sighing, bleeding, dying by the hundreds."

Lillian raised her eyebrows at Gabriel at the lines from the carol making their way back in.

"One wounded soldier, separated from his battalion, and sick of the war, decides that come what may, he *would* be home for Christmas. So, at the twilight's last gleaming, he packed up his old kit-bag, and headed out over lonesome no-man's-land."

Gabriel took a few steps backwards and, with a dramatic flourish, waved his hand to the action. "That's the Prologue. The Epilogue is shorter."

"Let me see that." Lillian reached for the script and glanced over it. "But – some of these lines are clearly borrowed."

"Yeah," said Gabriel. "We wanted it to sound old-fashioned. Kind of poetic."

"Well – I think perhaps they're too recognizable. 'The twilight's last gleaming?'"

"Billy added that line. Should I change it?"

"And some of these other phrases…"

"You think we have to start over?"

Lillian saw the disappointment in his face, the worry in Tommy's.

"No. Overall, it's very good. But – I think you should change some of the borrowed lines. You could keep a word here or there, but I think it would be better to make it your own."

"Okay, we'll change those parts," said Gabriel. "Here's the Epilogue. Tell me what you think."

Tommy sat up, and continued to crack his knuckles. "Remember, Gabe, you have to memorize this part. You can't mess up."

"Right." Gabriel again took center stage. He peered into the distance. "From yonder light – "

"No, Gabriel! We changed it. 'Across the seas…'"

"Oh, yeah. I forgot."

Tommy plopped on the couch. "You have to get it right, Gabriel. The ending is the most important part of the whole play!" He turned to Lillian. "He's not taking it seriously enough."

"Yes, I am." He leaned in towards Lillian, cupped his hand around his mouth and spoke in a loud vaudevillian stage whisper. "Dis guy worries 'bout everyting!" Gabriel rummaged around in his mind, moving his fingers along the words. "Got it." He cleared his throat in a trumpet-like manner, and waved his arms dramatically over the imaginary scenes.

"Across the seas, across the fields, our brave hero finally reaches the ole farm. And from afar, yon light shines brightly, the golden windows welcoming him home." In another stage whisper he added, "Amy wrote that part."

"Come on, Gabriel! Stick to your lines!" said an increasingly worried Tommy.

"All right, all right." He slipped back into character. "Around the hearth sits his wife and children, stringing popcorn for the Christmas tree. The soldier knocks at the door," Gabriel paused expectantly, and rapped on the coffee table. "And his *youngest* son opens the door. Then the soldier says: 'I'm home, dearest family! I'm finally home!' Then I face the audience, throw open my arms and say: 'A very Merry Christmas to you all!'"

"That's wonderful!" said Lillian, clapping. "The epilogue is perfect. You don't need to change a word. Your father's going to love it! The detail about the family decorating the tree is really good." She rubbed Tommy's shoulder in encouragement. "Well done, boys!"

Tommy was torn between skepticism and pride. "It needs a little more work, and – "

"Hey, how about we get *our* tree?" asked Gabriel. "We could have it all decorated by the time Dad gets here. He'll be just like the hero, coming home for Christmas."

Tommy lit up at the idea. "Can we, Mom? Now?" he asked.

"Now?" asked Lillian. She glanced at the clock. "It's a school night."

"Can we?" said Gabriel, catching her hesitation. "Please?"

Lillian jumped to her feet. "All right! Let's go get our tree for our returning hero!"

Tommy and Gabriel exchanged glances of amazement, and then ran to put on their coats.

Chapter 10

By mid-week, Ed and Jimmy were laying out the plans for whitewashing. Ed squinted at the sky and rubbed his chin. "Change is on the way. Knew the mild weather couldn't last much longer. Good thing we're starting on this today."

"The way these crazy dang Krauts work, I wouldn't be surprised if we finish it in a few days."

Ed gave a chuckle at the low estimation. "It won't take them that long. Gustav has experience. Has a farm of his own, you know."

Jimmy didn't want to admit to being impressed by the Germans. He kept a cool detachment, and tried to hate them. But the more he worked with them, the more they reminded him of his brothers – good-natured, serious in many ways, hard-working. And he was keenly aware of the respect they showed to everyone, especially his mother. He couldn't deny that the farm needed them and that they were helping to make it a success.

Ed and Jimmy mixed the lime and water into two batches, and Otto began giving instructions to the prisoners. The POWs kept on one side of the barn all morning, climbing into the rafters and the loft to paint, while Ed and Jimmy worked on the other side.

When Ursula came out with coffee mid-morning, she noticed Jimmy observing the prisoners from his side of the barn. She saw him try to hide a smile at Karl's playful clowning. Karl, with his big grin and boyish energy, was impossible not to like. She could see that Jimmy was pleased at the progress, and she breathed a sigh of relief. Jimmy seemed willing to tolerate the prisoners, and kept his animosity towards Friedrich hidden.

Ursula knew she wouldn't have a chance to speak to Friedrich, and though she longed for him, she was reluctant to even look his way. Ed's earlier comment had startled her; if Ed understood that there was something between them, then they had not been as careful as she had believed. She checked on the attention of everyone, and seeing that they were all occupied, she turned her eyes to Friedrich. She caught him looking at her, and her heart melted. One brief moment of understanding, and then they both averted their gaze. And yet it was like food to her starving soul. That look of tenderness would sustain her for days, weeks. His eyes had reached out and caressed her, comforted her, and that sweetness had settled deep inside. Her face softened, the tension left her limbs, and a small place for happiness spread in her mind, like a patch of grass where she could rest and take in the warmth of the sun.

She and Jessica delivered their lunch at noon, and stayed to chat with Jimmy. The prisoners took ten minutes, and then went right back to work. Ursula hoped this joint task would lessen Jimmy's hostility towards them. But just as she and Jessica were leaving, Jimmy crossed to where the POWs were working. Ursula's heart began to beat in dread. Karl was just about to finish covering the dingy brown wall with whitewash.

"Karl!" Jimmy cried and walked over to him. "Wait."

Everyone froze. It was the first time Jimmy had spoken directly to any of the POWs.

Karl looked up in surprise, his paint brush dripping.

Jimmy took a small brush and dipped it into Karl's bucket. He painted a two-foot horizontal line across the weathered wood. Karl watched him, unsure of what he meant. Then Jimmy drew an elongated loop below it, and two half-circles resting on the line. Karl tilted his head in puzzlement, and set his bucket down. Then Jimmy added hands and the eyes, and below the drawing wrote *Kilroy was here.*

Karl took a step back, and saw the cartoon of a man peeking over a fence. He burst into laughter.

"Gustav! *Kommen Sie hier!*" he said, waving the older POW over. He pointed to the drawing. "Friedrich, look! Kilroy *vass* here!" He laughed again, his hands on his knees, while Ed, Otto, and then Jessica also went to see.

Jessica clapped her hands and took the paintbrush from Karl. She painted a frame around the drawing. "This stays! Don't anyone paint over it. Tell them, Otto." Otto translated her message to the Germans, while Jimmy went back to his side of the barn, gratified by Ursula's gentle smile of approval.

She knew it was Jimmy's way of promising a truce, while he was home.

*

A working camaraderie had been established between Jimmy and the prisoners. They had gone from being hateful Nazis, to despicable Krauts, to Germans, to POWs alone and far from home. It hadn't been easy, for any of them, but they had won Jimmy's respect, and were carrying out his plans for the farm. The barn was whitewashed, the repairs were almost completed on the outbuildings, and Jimmy had even found time to make the arbor for Kate's garden and the gate for the picket fence.

And yet, Ursula noted, Friedrich and Jimmy stayed away from each other. Though it pained her, she believed that at least a conflict would be avoided this way.

Relations further softened after Gustav and Karl helped Jimmy and Jessica find and bring home a Christmas tree. Friedrich had declined, saying he would work with Ed on the machines that needed some maintenance. Ursula knew that the tradition would be too painful for him to participate in, too much of a reminder of his loss. Even Gustav and Karl went from laughing and singing as they brought the tree home to a wistful sadness when the tree was carried inside the house.

In the late afternoon, Ursula stepped into the barn to let Jimmy know that Gladys had called for him. He was putting down fresh hay for the cows; Otto and Friedrich were on the other side of the barn, filling up the trough with feed. Jimmy began to leave, then hesitated a moment.

Ursula filled with dread as Jimmy crossed the barn and approached Friedrich. Otto raised his head and exchanged a look of concern with her.

Friedrich flinched on finding Jimmy suddenly next to him, and awaited some new confrontation.

Jimmy took a moment, and kicked at the straw. Then he looked up and spoke quietly. "I'm sorry for your loss. I am. That's, that's – " He gave up trying to find words. No hand was offered, just the words. Then he turned and went to the house.

Ursula saw Friedrich's body sag, as if tension alone had been holding him up against his grief. He leaned on the stall and his head dropped. If Otto had not been there, she would have run to him.

She saw her mother walking down the lane to check on the mail and went out to join her. Jessica usually brought the mail, but Kate had been checking it more and more. Ursula knew it was her desire to know about Eugene – and her determination to face the truth.

There was no news, no letter about Eugene. Ursula linked her arm with Kate's and talked about the dinner they were making that night for Gladys, who would be joining them.

Spirits rose that evening at what turned into an impromptu tree-trimming party. Jessica begged

Jimmy and Gladys to help her decorate the tree after dinner. They had just started stringing the lights when Joe Madden, Sue Ellen, and Shirley stopped by and were only too happy to help with the tree.

Kate came to life, providing hot cider and a plate of ginger bread. Sue Ellen played Christmas music on the piano, singing gleefully to her own accompaniment, with Gladys, Jessica, and Shirley joining in from time to time. Sometimes they stood behind her, with ornaments or a garland in their hands, or one of them would find another song in the music book for her to play.

Later, sitting in front of the lit tree, Kate and Gladys talked about the civilian defense projects that Gladys's mother and aunt were heavily involved with. And Sue Ellen and Shirley described the plans for their Christmas party and took a vote on whether they should add cocktail franks or Swedish meatballs to the mix of appetizers and sandwiches.

And once, amid the merriment, Ursula and Jimmy caught each other's eye and smiled at the happiness all around them.

*

On Friday, despite the vying sources of anxiety within her, Ursula felt inexplicably happy. Jimmy was exactly like his old self all morning – playful and spontaneous, laughing with Ed about old times. She knew he was happy to be seeing Gladys again that evening, but he was also friendlier with the Germans, even taking his lunch in the machine shed with them and Otto while they discussed the last of the repairs with Ed.

After lunch, Otto and Ed took Gustav and Karl to deliver the cord of wood to Mrs. England, leaving Jimmy and Friedrich to finish up on the machine shed repairs. Ursula could barely suppress the bubble of happiness inside her. Jimmy and Friedrich appeared to have buried the hatchet. They had worked all morning on repairs to the loft and were now, together, returning the various tools and machine parts to the loft.

Jessica had just gathered up the lunch plates and headed to the house. She would be busy all afternoon helping Kate with the baking, and with Gladys on her way over, Ursula thought she might finally find a few moments to be alone with Friedrich. There had been no opportunity for them to speak alone and her heart was aching for him. She watched him work from the other side of the shed. His sleeves were rolled up; she looked at his muscular forearms and remembered his embraces. Her eyes traveled over his dark hair, his neck and shoulders, and she remembered her hands in his hair, holding his face, covering his mouth with kisses.

Jimmy stood on a ladder, handing the last of the parts up to Friedrich in the loft. They were nearly done. Jimmy looked around and smiled at Ursula. "Never thought we'd get it all done."

She knew that was as close to a compliment that he would give to Friedrich. But it was enough to make her smile.

"I'll move the tractor outside, and then we can finish up with those shelves," said Jimmy.

"I can move it," Ursula said. "Finish what you're doing."

Perhaps it was her happiness at seeing Jimmy working side by side with Friedrich, or her mind being pulled in several directions, but for one brief moment, Ursula lost her concentration.

She had started the tractor countless times, always careful of the kickback of the hand crank. But today, with an eye on Friedrich and Jimmy, she dropped her guard. While cranking the engine, it kicked and the crank flew out, slamming her hand against the wall and causing her to fall. She shrieked in pain, and held her bleeding hand.

"Ursula!" cried Friedrich. In a flash, he swung down from the loft and ran to her side. He dropped to his knees and clasped her arm. He put another hand to her cheek. "Ursula! Are you – "

She raised her eyes to him, her face filled with tender sorrow – and he realized what he was doing. He squeezed his eyes shut and groaned at his mistake.

Jimmy gripped the sides of the ladder, stunned, and stared in disbelief. Seething with outrage, he climbed off the ladder and walked over to them.

Ursula slowly rose to her feet. She protectively stepped in front of Friedrich, admitting her guilt, and met Jimmy's glare.

Jimmy's fists clenched at his sides, and in a voice husky with anger he spoke in a low, barely controlled hiss. "So that's how it is." He turned to Friedrich. "You son of a bitch."

Friedrich remained on his knees and buried his face in his hands. Ursula kept her eyes on Jimmy, waiting for him to lash out.

He lifted her hand and inspected it. "Get in the truck."

"Jimmy, please – "

"I said get in the truck! Now! You're gonna need stitches." He loomed over Friedrich. "I'll deal with you later."

Jessica had heard the scream and now ran back into the barn. "What happened?"

She covered her mouth on seeing Ursula's bloody hand. "Oh my God! Ursula!" She glanced down at Friedrich, then up at Jimmy.

Jimmy pulled out his handkerchief and began to bind Ursula's hand. "Go tell Mom I gotta take my stupid sister to get stiches. Call Doc Morris and tell him we're on our way. Go on!" He pulled on Ursula's good arm and led her to the truck.

Jessica followed them. "I'm going with you."

Jimmy shoved his finger in the air at her. "No, you're not! You stay here and tell Mom what happened."

Jessica hesitated, looking to Ursula for some direction. But Ursula simply climbed into the truck, and stared out at the horizon.

"Just do as I say!" Jimmy yelled, slamming the door after Ursula.

Jessica followed him to his side of the truck. "What should I tell Mom?"

Jimmy couldn't look at Ursula. Or Jessica. He stared at the steering wheel, then turned on the engine. "Tell her that her fool of a daughter made a big mistake."

The entire ride into town, Jimmy cursed under his breath, cursed his sister, cursed Friedrich, cursed the POWs, cursed the German army, cursed the war. Ursula sat stoically, ignoring all his remarks, ignoring the pain in her hand, and focused her eyes ahead of her.

Jimmy sped along the country road, slowing only when he came into town. He squealed to a stop when he arrived at the doctor's office. Then he jumped out of the truck, opened Ursula's door, and led her inside where they were expecting her. Jimmy waited outside, pacing up and down the sidewalk.

Half an hour later, Ursula came out with her hand in stitches and her arm in a sling. Jimmy exchanged a few words with the doctor, who assured Jimmy she would be fine.

They got back into the truck. Jimmy kept muttering and cursing, now and then turning to look over at Ursula's pale, tear-streaked face.

Once they were out of town, he broke his silence, his voice strained with low, overly-controlled words.

"How long has this been going on?"

Ursula couldn't speak. Her mouth started to tremble.

"How long?" he demanded.

Ursula's words came out in a whisper. "A year." Then sorrow filled her eyes. "I didn't mean for it to happen. I tried to hate him. I did hate him. But I – "

Jimmy pounded the steering wheel. "I should have killed the bastard. I'm going to beat the living daylights out of him – "

"No!" Ursula turned on him like a wild cat, taking him by surprise. "Don't you dare lay a finger on him, Jimmy! Don't you dare! You stay away from him – don't you so much as touch him!"

He stared in disbelief at the fire in her face, the flash in her eyes. In an instant, her timid regret was replaced with the threatening strength of a wounded animal protecting its cubs. Jimmy realized he was up against some primal force that far outstripped his anger. He turned his gaze back to the road.

Though Ursula was trying to hold herself together, the floodgates inside were bulging to the point of breaking. The months of damming up her anguish, of hiding her predicament, of keeping everything to herself, finally overwhelmed her, and she allowed the gates to burst open. There was nothing left to lose. She broke down into unrestrained sobbing.

Jimmy waited for her to stop, but instead it grew worse, deeper. She, who used to pride herself on being tough and never crying, was now sobbing uncontrollably. He tried to keep his eyes on the road, but kept looking over at her, growing worried.

"Jesus Christ, what's wrong with you, Ursula?" He wondered if she could hurt herself with such hard crying. "Okay, okay," he finally said. "You made a mistake and – "

"Don't you dare touch him, Jimmy!"

"Okay. I won't hurt him," he said, unnerved by her passion. He tried to regain the upper hand. "But he's leaving our farm."

"No! Leave him alone! Leave us alone!"

Jimmy jerked his head to face her. She wasn't backing down; if anything, she appeared ready to battle him to the end. He had never seen her like this, so uncontrolled, so full of despair.

"If anything happens to him, I'll never forgive you! Never!"

She was like a storm of fury and anguish, surprising him with unexpected gusts and startling strikes of lighting.

"Get a grip, Ursula. What the hell's wrong with you?"

"I love him! Yes, I love him. And I'm going to marry him. I don't care what anyone says." She broke down again into deep sobs, offering no excuse, no explanation, just letting the months of torment shake her body as the tears streamed down her face.

Jimmy kept one hand on the steering wheel and with the other he tried to make a gesture of calm. "Okay, Ursula. Okay." He took a deep breath. "But pull yourself together. You're going to make yourself sick." He searched for a reasonable solution for the time being. "You – You're just going to have to wait. Until after the war. Nothing else can be done now. Surely you see that."

"I can't wait," she said in a choking voice, and burst anew into sobs.

Everything he said only made it worse; if anything, her crying became more desperate.

"This isn't normal, Ursula. Get a hold of yourself! You've been acting strange ever since I got here. All distracted and secretive. Now this."

Jimmy shifted his eyes from the road to Ursula, waiting for some explanation. "What's going on with you?"

Ursula checked her sobs, and seemed to gain some composure. She turned her tear-streaked face to him, and met his eyes. "What do you think?"

He looked back out at the road, his eyebrows pinched. Then, like an explosion in his brain, he was struck with understanding, and jerked his head to her.

Ursula held his gaze, and calmly nodded.

Jimmy slammed on the brakes, and pounded the steering wheel. "Jesus Christ! Don't tell me – Jesus Christ!"

He got out of the truck, slammed the door, and used language Ursula had never heard him use before. He kicked at the ground, cursing everything and everyone. He pounded the hood, then kicked at the tire. He walked several yards ahead of the truck, then back. He threw up his hands and clenched them at the sky. And walked several yards behind the truck. He opened the door, changed his mind and slammed it shut, and cursed some more. Then he stood still, staring at the road, and shook his head.

Finally, he opened the door, climbed inside, and slammed the door.

"This is what I come home to? What in the hell were you thinking? How could you? You of all people. I thought you hated the Germans. You wanted to go after them yourself when Francy was killed. For God's sake, did you think about what Francy would – "

"Don't say it, Jimmy! Please don't say anything! I didn't mean for it to happen. I didn't mean for you to find out. I wanted to hide it from you. I don't want to burden anyone else with this."

He turned to her, incredulous. "It's not like this is something you can hide! Who else knows? Does Mom know?"

Ursula whipped her head up. "No! No one knows." She broke down and cried so hard that Jimmy started to feel bad. He took a deep breath, and tried to think of what to do.

"She'll find out soon enough, Ursula."

"I can't tell her. Not while Eugene – " She couldn't finish her sentence.

"Does Jessica know?"

"No! No one knows, Jimmy." Her mouth began to tremble. "Not even Friedrich."

His eyes widened in disbelief, and then he slumped, his fury gone. "Aw hell, Ursula. You kept this to yourself?"

"Who could I tell?" she asked, raising her face. "I can't let anyone know. I don't want them to take him away." And with that she burst into fresh sobs.

Jimmy gently patted her shoulder. "Stop crying, Ursula. Please, stop. It's not – it's not good for you."

He looked at her swollen eyes and wet face and felt a rush of love for her. "My stupid, brave sister. Going through this all on your own."

Ursula's sobs lessened and she tried to talk through her ragged breathing. "At first I thought –

I thought of going to Aunt Lillian's. When it got closer. So I wouldn't have to face anyone here."

"And then what? Just come home with a baby?"

"I know, I know. It was a stupid idea."

They were silent for several moments. "Listen. You have to see a doctor about this."

Ursula lifted her sleeve to her face and wiped at her eyes. "I already have. That's why I've been going to Peoria. I couldn't go to anyone around here."

Jimmy looked at her afresh, amazed at her fortitude, how she had kept it hidden. He tried to imagine what she was going through.

"Ursula. Do you – " He had to take a deep breath and blow it out. "Do you love him? I mean – do you really want to marry him?"

Again, her eyes filled with the fire of determination. "I *am* going to marry him. I don't care how long it takes."

Jimmy read her face, and believed her. He fixed his eyes on the road, and ransacked his head for possible solutions. He'd run with one idea and then abandon it in search for another. Again and again he came up empty.

Ursula saw the struggle in her brother and softened towards him. "Jimmy. I know he is German. I know he is – the enemy. But he's a good man. He is."

"Okay. Just – let me think." He put his fist to his mouth and stared out the window. "Let's keep it quiet for now. How long – when – "

"April. Mid-April. I'll be showing soon."

"Well you can't hide it much longer. People will know."

"Everyone thinks I have a beau in Peoria. Let them go on thinking that. Please. I couldn't bear it if he were taken away. Or punished." She broke into fresh tears.

"Okay. But we gotta get you married."

"To him."

"Well then you better tell him."

She pressed her fingers to her forehead. "I know. I wanted to. He was gone when I found out. When it was confirmed. They were all taken to work on the levee. He was gone for so long. For six weeks. Then when he came back he had the news about his family. I just couldn't add to his sorrow."

"Jesus Christ, Ursula," he said softly. He looked at his little sister – beautiful, strong, willful Ursula – and was amazed at both her strength and fragility. Just like their mother. Strong on the outside, all sweetness and love on the inside. His heart melted for her. "We'll figure something out, Ursula. You hear me? I'm – I'm on your side."

He started to put his arm around her but she winced in pain and held her arm. "Sorry. I gotta get you home. Don't worry. I'll think of something."

She smiled softly in gratitude. But the look of dismay on his face let her know that he didn't have a clue about what could be done. He started the truck and they drove in silence.

Ursula had been staring out the window, trying to decide whether to tell Jimmy what was on her mind. "Jimmy, do you remember what Ed said about the POWs marrying *in absentia*? I've been thinking that maybe we can make it work for us."

Jimmy's head snapped up at the absurdity of the suggestion. "You'd have to have an address in Germany! And who's going to vouch for you? You know someone there who would impersonate you? Use your head, Ursula."

She didn't want to let on how she had pinned her impossible hopes on that tiny bit of information she had heard. She had spun an improbable plan, because she could think of nothing else. The tears began to fall again, on realizing the futility of her situation.

"Try to pull yourself together for now. You hear me?"

She nodded. "Can you stop the truck?" she asked, wiping at her face. "I – I want to walk a bit. I can't let Mom see me like this."

Jimmy pulled over. Then, seeing that she was struggling with the handle, he reached over and opened her door. She stepped out, and walked up and down the side of the road, taking deep shaky breaths. Then she crossed over the ditch, and leaned against the wooden fence. He watched her gaze off at the horizon. A flock of crows lifted from the barren field and cawed against the sunset sky. As the sun dropped below the horizon, all warmth seemed to leave the day.

He stepped out and joined her at the fence. "Come on. I need to get you home. You – you have to start taking care of yourself now."

She lifted her face to him. "Thank you, Jimmy." She briefly rested her head against his chest and he patted her shoulder. Then she took a deep breath, as if steeling herself, and walked back to the truck. She struggled in frustration with her arm, and climbed awkwardly onto the seat. Jimmy closed the door after her, and they drove home.

They weren't ready for Kate's fury when they arrived home. They both feared that she had somehow found out. Was it possible that the doctor had noticed and called her?

Ursula saw the tiger inside her mother crouched and waiting to pounce. She plopped down into the kitchen chair and passively awaited the attack.

Jimmy tried to cover for her. "She needed a couple of stitches, but she'll be all right in a few days." He glanced at Jessica for a clue to Kate's anger, but couldn't read her face.

"Well, I'm glad to hear it!" Kate stomped around the kitchen, banging things as she fixed a strong cup of tea for Ursula. Every now and then she cast a look of outrage at Ursula. "Drink this," she said, setting the cup of tea on the table.

Ursula took the cup, and wrapped her hands around it.

Kate stood next to the table and crossed her arms, her anger clearly directed at Ursula. She let Ursula take a few sips, but couldn't contain her outrage any longer. "Guess who I had a call from?"

Ursula looked up to her mother. Then over to Jessica. Then back to her mother.

"Mildred Bloomfield. To tell me that she ran into Dolores's mother who happens to be in town visiting. And that Dolores has been working up in Seneca at the shipyard. Since October!" She waited for Ursula to say something, but she remained silent. Kate dropped her arms in disbelief. "You lied to me? I can't believe a daughter of mine would blatantly lie to my face! Let alone what you were really doing up there in Peoria! What do you have to say for yourself? Ursula!"

She waited for Ursula to speak, but she simply stared into her tea cup.

"Stubborn girl!" Kate threw the dish towel onto the counter. "You are *not* going to Peoria again. Do you hear me?" She began busying herself with the pans of food on the stove, opening lids, and then slamming them shut. "You can be sure that Mildred and Sue Ellen will broadcast the news to the entire town!"

Ursula exchanged a look with Jimmy, and then shut her eyes. Ashamed and hurt as she was, she felt a wave of relief. No more tiresome train rides to Peoria. No more lonesome nights in the train station, waiting for morning.

Kate noticed that Ursula had gone pale. "Are you all right?" She looked over at Jimmy. "What did the doctor say?"

"Just that she needs to rest," said Jimmy.

Kate was smitten with remorse. "We can discuss all this later. Jessica, carry her tea upstairs for her. Come, Ursula." She placed a hand under her good arm. "Come. You need to rest for now." She smoothed her hand over her daughter's hair, and gently walked with her up the stairs.

Chapter 11

❧

Gabriel had introduced Lillian to Henry at the hospital, and she had since spoken with him several times. Though her role as instructor for Artists for Victory didn't intersect with Henry's in the recreation room, she made a point of getting to know him better, and she found him a charming man.

She had often observed that most volunteers tended to be at ease with a particular age group, or perhaps rank, or degree of recovery; but Henry was equally comfortable with all the patients – and was a favorite with the nurses. He had a way of adding a little cheer and humor to the goings-on, and he often sat with the wounded veterans one-on-one, encouraging them in their journey ahead. Lillian knew that it was beneficial for the patients to interact with different ages, old and young. Volunteers like Gabriel and Henry helped to create an atmosphere closer to what the wounded GIs would be going home to.

Tonight, after her class, Lillian met Henry and Gabriel in the rec room and observed Henry as he coached a young patient for the table tennis tournament. Lillian was surprised at Henry's nimbleness. He had to be well into his seventies, but he moved with the sprightliness of a young man. Several of the patients cheered them on. Gabriel was glued to the exchange, and Lillian could see that he was eager to play.

When the match finished, Henry waved him over to the table. "Come on, Gabriel. You're up. Give Sergeant Buchols a run for his money – and don't go easy on him!"

Gabriel held his own against the soldier for a few serves, but when the balls landed closer and closer to the edges of the table, Gabriel found himself lurching from one side to the other in order to hit the ball. In one valiant reach, he smacked the ball with the tip of his paddle. It bounced off the ceiling light fixture and hit Gabriel smack on the forehead, causing all the men, and Gabriel himself, to explode into laughter.

"Okay, men," said Henry, lifting the tin box of prize money. "You've only got a few days to practice." He shook the box tantalizingly, and then handed it to the rec room coordinator.

Henry rode the bus back with Lillian and Gabriel. He was going to join the final rehearsal at Mrs. Kuntzman's. There had been two stage rehearsals at school, and the performance was on Saturday.

"You will be there, won't you, Henry?" asked Lillian.

"Wouldn't miss it for the world. And I'll be escorting Martha. Mrs. Kuntzman, that is."

Lillian smiled at his slip. "And my friend Izzy will be there," she added. "And I'm expecting Charles to arrive tomorrow or Saturday morning. So you'll all get to meet one another."

"Sounds just dandy," said Henry. "Should be quite a show, with this one here," he elbowed Gabriel, "getting the last line of the whole she-bang." He opened the small bag on his lap, checked on its contents, and then winked at Gabriel.

Lillian looked on with curiosity.

"Raisins. Golden raisins for Mrs. Kuntzman. Took me a week to find them. Went all over the city. But I found them, all right. She'll be pleased." He smiled at the vision of handing the bag to her.

Gabriel clasped his hands and slipped into Mrs. Kuntzman's character: "Mein Gott im Himmel! Golden raisins for mien apfelstrudle. Such a good man! Your Oma vould be proud!"

Henry burst out laughing. "That's her to a T. Always praising everybody. Lovely quality, that. And Gabriel and Billy, why, they can imitate anyone."

"Indeed, they can," said Lillian. Over the past year, Gabriel had become much more outgoing, and thankfully, had abandoned his solitary "explorer" phase. For the most part, she credited this change with Billy's entertaining company, and the simple fact that Gabriel was growing up.

Gabriel and Billy found great fun in doing impersonations and little impromptu skits in different accents, different characters. When Billy visited for rehearsals, Lillian was often impressed by the exactness of their mimicry and the spontaneity of their acts. They sometimes stayed in character for the entire visit, exasperating Tommy and Mickey, and causing Lillian to turn aside to hide her laughter.

Lillian left Gabriel and Henry at the steps of Mrs. Kuntzman's. Their old babysitter stood in the doorway, wearing her red poinsettia holiday apron, and waving them inside. "I made chicken pot pie for youse all! Come in, come in!"

In the window, Tommy, Mickey, Amy, and Billy were motioning for them to hurry – no doubt as a result of the enticing aroma coming from the kitchen.

Lillian entered her apartment building and hurried to her mailbox – and found what she had hoped to find. A letter from Charles. She opened it on the spot. Just a few lines, saying he would be home soon, and that he loved her. In half a page he managed to write that he loved her three times.

She breathed a sigh of relief and realized that she had feared another delay. She went upstairs, fixed a quick meal, and relaxed in a hot bath. She mentally went over the dinners she had planned, the movies she wanted to see with Charles, and outings with the boys they could all take. She would have to be careful not to tax him. Most likely he had minimized his illness and might still need to rest. But he said he was looking forward to the trip upstate to Annette's. And then, the culmination of his visit – their early anniversary celebration.

Lillian towel dried her hair, slipped on her robe, and checked on the apartment. Everything was ready for Charles. The tree was up and decorated, the stockings hung from the mantel, the presents were wrapped. The bookshelves were filled with Christmas figurines and holiday school projects the boys had made over the years. After going from room to room, she decided to finish up on the quilt she had been working on. She wanted to stay busy to keep her excitement in check.

She took out her sewing basket and then curled up on the couch, humming along with the music from the radio. Soon she was adding the final touches to the quilt. She would put the backing on after Charles was gone. She would need something to fill those first awful days after he left. Each time it took her weeks to adjust to his absence, weeks to accept the fact that he was miles away. Weeks before his letters started to arrive.

For the first time in a long time, Lillian enjoyed the quiet time alone. There was a semblance of the way things used to be, before the world was shaken by war. She could almost pretend that the war was over; that Charles would be coming home soon from work.

She bit off the thread and then held up the quilt, delighted with the outcome. It was small and pretty, with a bit of embroidered flowers, vines, and leaves here and there. She felt a sweet tenderness for the quilt.

Soon, the vestibule door opened and closed, and she heard the voices and running feet of Tommy and Gabriel. Gabriel came in first, followed by Tommy, who wore a look of consternation.

"How was your rehearsal?"

"Just dandy," said Gabriel, taking off his jacket and casting a side glance at Tommy. "Well, the chicken pot pie was good, anyway."

She turned to Tommy for his response.

"We're a hundred percent ready, Mom, but Gabriel and Billy goofed off the whole time! Doing their lines as Laurel and Hardy, and Mo and Curly, and Jimmy Cagney."

Lillian raised her eyebrows at Gabriel.

He smiled impishly and shrugged. "You were laughing, too, Tommy.

"I couldn't help it! But you better not do it at the play."

"I know, I know. It's not a comedy!" he said, in exact imitation of Tommy. "Don't worry." He saw that the quilt she had been working on was folded. "Did you finish it, Mom?"

Lillian nodded and held it up. "What do you think, boys?"

Tommy frowned. "I hope that's not for us. It's too girly."

"Not to mention too small," added Gabriel. "Is it a baby blanket?"

Lillian assessed it anew, and then refolded it. "I was just using up some remnants. I'll find some use for it." She put her scissors, needle, and thread back into her sewing basket. "I'll finish it later. I'll have time after your father leaves."

"Or maybe you won't," said Tommy. "You might be doing drawings for that art director."

Lillian laughed. "Yes, maybe I will. I think I would enjoy that."

"Then I hope it happens," said Gabriel, sitting by her side.

Tommy sat on her other side, cracking his knuckles. "Are you sure Dad will be home in time for the play?"

"He'll be here," said Lillian. "He sent a letter saying he would leave Saturday morning, and expects to be here in the afternoon. He can't wait to see it!"

Tommy got up and plugged in the Christmas tree lights. Then Gabriel ran to turn off the overhead light.

"It's more Christmassy this way," he said.

They all looked at the Christmas tree, its soft light and shining ornaments adding a bit of magic to the night.

"I'm glad Dad will be here," said Tommy. "It just didn't feel right last year."

Lillian put her arms around the boys. "No, it didn't. But this year will be different. He will be here for three whole weeks!"

"Do you think he'll like what we got for him at The Red String Curio Store?" asked Gabriel, going to the tree and looking at the presents.

"The box with the ship on it? I know he will!"

Gabriel lifted a few presents and read the tags on them. "Hey! I didn't see this one. It has my name on it." He gently shook it and tried to gauge the weight. "Can I have a hint?"

"Absolutely not! You'd be sure to guess what it was."

Tommy was now checking out the presents, looking for any new ones. "Here's one for me!" His eyes lit up. "Here's another one for you, Gabe."

Lillian watched the boys and imagined that soon Charles would be by her side, watching the boys in their excitement. He would squeeze her hand, and she would know exactly what he meant: we have everything. There is nothing more that could possibly increase our happiness. And she would squeeze his hand back in agreement.

*

Charles rested peacefully, his last night at headquarters before going home. He was happy the meetings and reports and traveling were behind him. The trip to Washington and passing through the wholesome towns and countryside of Virginia had been unsettling in a strange way. He was over-whelmed by both a sense of gratitude, and something akin to guilt. He couldn't help but compare the destruction of Europe to the verdant beauty of the United States. Having seen the bleeding and wreckage of the cities in Europe, he was at first disconcerted by the absence of fighting — no air-raid sirens, no bombed-out buildings, no makeshift hospitals. And though there was rationing, people were eating and were well-fed.

In addition, he was taken aback by how crowded Washington had become, though he had heard of the chaos of such wartime boom towns – Mobile, Detroit, San Francisco, San Diego – crowds everywhere, people sleeping in shifts in the same rented beds, traffic jams. The catchphrase heard over and over was that everyone had more money, but there was less to spend it on. And yet people were spending left and right. Night life was booming, with long lines outside of restaurants, movie theaters, and dance halls.

Yet underneath the frenzy, he had noticed a shift in attitude everywhere he went. People were worn down by wartime living. He felt it himself. It seemed everyone had lost someone. He thought of his sister, Kate, and his heart sank – one son killed, another one missing. Like everyone, he just wanted it all to be over. And yet he had a sinking feeling in the pit of his stomach at what awaited him – a long, drawn-out battle with Japan, years of brutal fighting.

This war was different from his experience in the Great War. All war was horrible, a degradation to mankind – but this one was different. Or rather, he was different. He was a man now, not a boy. With a family. With Lillian. For so much of his life, he had abandoned the personal life. After the tragic death of his little brother and sister, and his mother's decline afterwards, he had joined the Navy, and later immersed himself in business. He had ignored the importance of relationships, love, and family – until he met Lillian.

He reached for her letters and pressed them to his chest. Now, the personal life was the only thing that mattered. He couldn't believe his good fortune at having found her, of having found love later in life; he suppressed all fears of ever losing that.

He read her most recent letter again. He didn't like the repeated mention of Henry. Henry would be at the play. Henry had been such a help with everything. Henry had a heart of gold. She couldn't wait for him to meet Henry.

Charles's heart shrunk at the praise, and he couldn't help but think of the broken hearts of the men who received Dear John letters. But then his heart swelled at her closing words of tenderness.

He rubbed his head. It was hard to sort out what was real, what was unreal. The world was both horrible and hopeful, people loved and…

He folded the letter and slid it back into the envelope. He would meet the handsome, young man, this Henry person. The man who must have hopes in Lillian; how could anyone not desire her? Let the man hope; he would hope in vain. Charles knew that he had Lillian's heart, and, at the most, she had befriended a fellow volunteer. Nothing more. It could be nothing more than that.

He fell asleep with her letter in his hands.

*

Lillian's anxiety grew as the day wore on and there was still no sign of Charles. He had called from Norfolk to say the trains were backed up. She knew the supply trains took precedence and the countryside was full of them.

On reflection, she thought that he had sounded quiet, sad even. Perhaps she shouldn't have taunted him with information about Henry. She was sorry she had said anything at all, and now she feared he might have taken her words more seriously than she had intended.

She glanced at the clock, but couldn't risk waiting any longer. The boys would be so disappointed if he missed the play. She had given Charles the time and location and they agreed that he would go straight to the school and meet them there if it got to be too late. She left her apartment and hastened to the high school.

A group of carolers were performing outside the auditorium, next to a War Bonds table. When Lillian looked around, she saw that the decorations had turned out beautifully. The hallway and auditorium were strung with streamers, and posted on the walls were various art projects by the different grades.

Tommy, dressed in his costume, had spotted her and ran up to meet her, with an expression of worry. "Where's Dad?"

"The trains are all backed up. He's doing his best to get here on time."

Tommy's face fell.

Lillian placed her hands on his shoulders. "Look at you! So handsome in your uniform. You'll have to keep it on for your father to see." He grinned his half smile, and then ran back to the stage. She saw him speak briefly to Gabriel, who also became crestfallen.

She entered the auditorium; it was quickly filling up. There was Izzy, waving her over to where she had saved two seats in the middle of a row. Mrs. Kuntzman and Henry sat on the end. She greeted them and was telling them about Charles's delay when the lights flicked off and on. She took her seat and exchanged a few words with Izzy.

"Isn't that Amy – Tommy's friend?" asked Izzy.

Lillian nodded. "Yes. She's the director of their play."

Izzy smiled at the authority Amy so easily carried as she managed last-minute details. "That girl is going to go far," she said. Then she let out a laugh as Billy poked his head out of the curtains, and was quickly yanked back in from behind.

While Lillian was facing Izzy, a young couple made their way into the row and took the empty seats next to hers. Lillian looked all around her for other open seats but didn't see any. She would keep her eye out for Charles, and if he arrived, she would join him at the back of the auditorium. The lights were lowered and the program began.

The carolers sang their way from one side of the auditorium to the other, while a few stragglers hurried to find seats, and the crowd settled down. The school principal came out and delivered a speech about the need for community and family and described several volunteer projects that were taking place over the holidays. Then he gave the podium to the drama teacher who thanked them all for coming, and read the list of performances. She read a poem from a soldier about Christmas and wartime. Finally, beaming with pride, she introduced the opening act.

When the first of the grade school skits began, Lillian leaned forward to see how her drawings had been implemented. She was delighted at the results of the costumes; the snow princesses, in particular, were absolutely charming. She kept checking for the arrival for Charles, but now it was too dark and crowded in the back to see anything. Even if he arrived, he would have a hard time locating her.

The grade school acts were followed by the skits of the junior high school classes, a ballet of sorts with mixed grades, and more singing. And then it was time for the grand finale. Lillian realized her palms were sweaty as the curtains parted. Tommy and Gabriel would be performing in front of so many people. She was suddenly nervous for them.

The lights dimmed and a spotlight shown on center stage. Gabriel strode into the light, carrying a script in one hand and a staff in the other. Izzy nudged Lillian. "How adorable! What is he – a doughboy Christmas spirit?"

Lillian wasn't sure how to answer. Gabriel seemed to have settled on a combination of Father Christmas, a doughboy, and The Grim Reaper. And the doughboy leggings that Billy had fashioned looked as if they belonged to a mummy.

Gabriel smiled out into the darkness, unrolled his script and held it up in front of him.

"Greetings family! Greetings friends! Welcome to all who have traversed from afar, over field and fountain – " He froze. He looked out at the audience, then back down at the script. He was holding the wrong script, the old one. He looked sideways to the curtains, and Lillian thought she could hear Tommy's scolding voice.

"Oh, no!" whispered Lillian, covering her mouth. Where was the correct script? Had he left it at home? Her heart began to beat faster.

When no one came out with the correct scroll, Gabriel cleared his throat and continued with his delivery of the lines from "We Three Kings" – but now he decided to sing them as well! "Field and fountain, moor, and mountain, following yonder star!"

Lillian knew how furious Tommy would be. What on earth was Gabriel doing?

Then Gabriel read the lines mixed with Shakespeare, deepening his voice in an exaggerated dramatic manner: "Our play tonight is about two soldiers, both alike in dignity, in awful Flanders, where we lay our scene. Cursed by an ancient grudge – "

"Shakespeare?" Izzy whispered. "Interesting."

Just when Lillian thought Gabriel was getting back on track, he switched to a Vaudevillian Brooklyn accent, the wise-guy character he and Billy were so fond of doing. His whole posture shifted along with the words: "and knee-deep in mud, dees guys are surrounded by trenches and barbed wire and whizzin' bullets." He dodged a few for effect.

Lillian heard a suppressed snort from Izzy, and twitters from the audience. The crowd was clearly amused by the entertainment.

Gabriel reverted to the dignified singing of the words from the carol: "In a world of gathering gloom. Sorrow, sighing, bleeding, dying – "holding the note, then back to the wise-guy – "by da hundreds. By da tousands!"

The audience's response now grew into freer laughter. After the seriousness of the other performances, they apparently welcomed this bit of clowning. Lillian couldn't help laughing, especially with Izzy letting loose in laughter next to her. From stage left, Lillian heard the words: "It's not a comedy!"

Gabriel threw his arms up to the auditorium and hollered, "It's not a comedy!" causing them to laugh all the more.

Then Gabriel grew solemn, and Lillian realized that he had full control over the crowd, making them laugh when he wanted, and grow quiet when he wanted.

He held up a hand. "One wounded soldier, separated from his battalion, and sick of the war, decided that come what may, he *would* be home for Christmas." Then, he delivered the last lines, switching between two melodies: "So at the twilight's last gleaming, he packed up his old kit-bag, and headed out over lonesome no-man's-land."

Then, resuming the seriousness of the play, he ad-libbed the final lines, dropping his voice almost to a whisper, until the audience was quiet, expectant.

"Over lonesome, deserted, dangerous, desolate no-man's-land. Awaiting whatever Fate had in store for him." He bent over, waving his arms in a dramatic flourish. He started to back up to stage right, but when he raised his eyes to the curtain, no doubt seeing Tommy, he changed course, and exited stage left.

The crowd howled at the prolonged exit, especially when Gabriel tripped over the wrapped leggings that had fallen around his ankles. He gathered them up in his arms, slung them over his shoulder, and marched off, making a couple of sharp pivots before exiting.

Izzy freely gave way to her enjoyment at Gabriel's antics, as did Henry.

Lillian breathed a sigh of relief when Mickey appeared on stage, followed by Tommy, still red in the face, but able to deliver his lines. They discussed missing their families at Christmas, with Mickey saying he had promised to be home this year. While Tommy returned to his men, Mickey climbed out of the trenches, and made his way across no-man's-land.

Then, a prolonged explosion – sound effects by Billy – caused Izzy, and several others, to burst anew into chuckling. Perhaps inspired by Gabriel's hamming it up, Billy tweaked his scene. When Mickey's character spotted the evil Jerry (Billy) at his back, he lurched to defend himself, with the intent of a clean (and well-rehearsed) bayonetting. Billy, however, dodged him – again and again. Mickey grew more and more exasperated with each thrust, and finally gave chase to Billy, who ducked and dodged around the stage, catapulting the audience into fresh laughter.

Mickey finally caught Billy by the collar, and muttered something under his breath to him. Billy threw up his arms, shrugged, and finally agreed to be bayonetted, at which point Mickey ran off.

But Billy wasn't quite finished. He opened one eye, to make sure his brother was gone, then, clasping his hands, he delivered an unscripted, "Mein Gott im Himmel!" causing Mrs. Kuntzman to utter a little cry of delight, and the audience to roar.

Billy then performed a long, agonizing death scene, beginning with several leg twitches, the lifting and dropping of his head, an attempt to crawl to the other side of the stage, then lying still until the twitching began again. As long as the audience laughed, Billy continued to twitch, roll, gasp, and groan.

Mickey finally also went off-script and stormed back onto no-man's-land. He grabbed Billy's legs and dragged the body off stage, with Billy waving goodbye – causing the audience to howl more than ever, and Izzy to bend over in laughter. Lillian had to wipe the tears from her cheeks, and from the corner of her eye she saw Henry slapping his knee and hooting in delight.

The rest of the play went more or less according to script, though Izzy, and by that time many in the audience, couldn't control their laughter at Billy's sound effects: bombs, bullets whizzing, thunder, gusts of wind – and his exaggerated tiptoe across the back of the stage, when he realized he was on the wrong side for his entrance as the fisherman.

When the scene shifted to the seashore, Billy appeared as an aged French fisherman and spotted the wounded soldier. This being his last scene, Billy pulled out all the stops. Izzy doubled over anew at the seashore sounds: waves crashing, a chorus of seagulls that went on for quite some time, and then the putt-putter of a motor boat, the sound clearly being made by the fisherman himself.

Billy sat behind a piece of cardboard with waves painted on its side and when he needed to motor towards the beach, he simply walked it over to where Mickey was frantically waving his arms to be saved. When he was finally pulled into the boat, Mickey poked Billy in the back – and the fisherman sped off, forcing the soldier to run to catch up with the boat.

The soldier finally made it to an Allied ship, and eventually sees the white cliffs of Dover. Without more ado, he disembarked, dropped to the sand and kissed it, and handed over the vital information to the intelligence officer. He then made his way to his farm – all valiantly enacted by Mickey. The soldier had made it home for Christmas.

The drama smoothly built up to the climax. Lillian was touched by the tenderness of the final scene, with the family sitting around the hearth, and the soldier making his way across the fields. In spite of the slapstick, it was a lovely story.

Gabriel once again took center stage, holding the bunch of holly that had come off his costume, and narrated the final scene. He gestured to the hero approaching his home. "Across the seas, across the fields, our hero finally reaches his farm. From afar yon light shone brightly, the golden window welcoming him home."

As Gabriel delivered his lines, he remembered to address the audience, scanning the crowd as if speaking directly to each.

"Around the hearth sat his wife and children, stringing popcorn to decorate the Christmas tree. He knocks – "

Billy's final sound effects went off without a hitch.

But Gabriel stood frozen.

Lillian broke out into a sweat. Now what?

Gabriel stared hard at the back of the auditorium.

Whispers from the curtains. "Gabriel! Your lines!"

"And! And!" came promptings from both sides of the stage.

"And," said Gabriel, taking a step forward and peering harder.

Tommy's urgent whispering grew into a holler from the curtains. "Gabriel!"

"And," stuttered Gabriel, "And – " He looked to the curtains, then back out at Charles. "And they lived happily ever after! DAD!" He tossed the holly, ran to the edge of the stage, leapt off, and tore down the aisle.

Lillian whipped around and saw Charles standing at the back. "Charles!"

She started to push through the row, stumbling over feet and knees.

Tommy took center stage and delivered the final lines: "And to all – A very Merry Christmas!"

Then he jumped down from the stage and ran to Charles. "Dad!"

By which point the audience was laughing and clapping, half at the play, half at the happy family embracing in the back.

Charles was overwhelmed with joy. That simple word, "Dad," coming from his dear sweet boys, holding him tight. And Lillian approaching – her joy matching his. There was Izzy. Was that Mrs. Kuntzman coming? There was the young man. All of them exiting their row. Almost in front of him.

Charles nodded to the handsome young man beside Lillian, ready to extend his hand. So, this was Henry. Charles smiled at the man, steeling his nerves – but the young man simply turned to the young woman at his other side and walked away.

Then Izzy shook his hand, and Mrs. Kuntzman welcomed him home. A whirlwind. An old man smiling at him, offering his hand.

"Dad, this is Henry!" Gabriel said.

That's Henry? Charles swallowed, overcome by happiness. He had to blink his eyes. What was wrong with him, he wondered? It was as if he had suddenly been granted his old life after seeing it slip away. Here was his family. They were together again.

"Charles!" Lillian said, embracing him.

And the world was set right.

Chapter 12

∾

The pain in Ursula's hand woke her in the early morning, and a fresh wave of shame washed over her – at the lie that had come between her and her mother. Ursula had always prided herself on being truthful, on having the courage to take responsibility for her actions. But this was different. She couldn't risk any harm or punishment coming to Friedrich.

And she worried that Jimmy was now involved – she worried for him. She had added another burden to his shoulders. The night before he had sat next to her bed, and for a moment she feared that he might have a change of heart, having had time to reconsider the gravity of her actions.

"You won't do anything to him, will you, Jimmy?" she had pleaded.

He had smiled, and for a moment she caught a glimpse of her old, sweet Jimmy, the soft-hearted boy he had always been. "Don't worry," he assured her. "I'll get along with them all. I can go back to hating after I leave."

He leaned forward and rested his elbow on his knees, squinting off at some internal vision.

"Hate is a slow poison, Ursula. I might have a temper, but I was never a hater. But with this war, I have to be. Otherwise, it just makes no sense. No sense." He remained silent for a while. Then he sat up straight, and the soldier in him returned. His face became older, full of authority and seriousness. "All that matters now is that you take care of yourself. You hear me?" She had nodded. And then he left her room.

Jessica had come in repeatedly to make sure Ursula had everything she needed, and to try to cheer her up. And, once, her mother had come.

Kate had scooted the chair closer to the bed and checked Ursula's hand to make sure there was no infection. Ursula felt the strain between them and kept her eyes on her mother.

"I'm sorry, Mom."

"What is it you're sorry for?" Kate said, fixing her with a stare that demanded nothing less than the truth.

Ursula met her eyes with the same level of honesty. "I'm sorry I lied to you."

"Is that all you have to be sorry about?"

Ursula looked down at her blanket and considered how to answer. There was only one way. "Yes. That's the only thing I'm sorry about."

Kate's stern mouth softened into a wry smile. "I know you're telling the truth. And yet I know there's more. And I know you won't tell me what it is until you're good and ready." She stood, let out a puff of frustration, and began to leave. Then she stopped at the door, and turned to Ursula. "And the reason I know that – is because I'm the exact same way."

The words, harsh in one sense, forgiving in another, had taken away some of the remorse at having lied to her mother. And yet they both understood that until Ursula was ready to talk, a distance would remain between them. A lie would sit between them where before there had always been truth.

Ursula dressed for the day, her hand slowing her down and making the simplest tasks difficult, like brushing her hair and pulling on her clothes. She had to keep the sling on to prevent her hand from throbbing.

Thank goodness for the Bloomfield's party this evening, she thought. It would provide a much-needed distraction for them all. Jimmy and Jessica would attend the party, leaving her and her mother alone for the evening. Ursula was happy for the excuse not to go. The idea of being around so much merriment, of pretending to be happy, was more than she could do.

And the party would finally give her a chance to see Friedrich. She would find a few minutes to slip out and talk with him. She stopped brushing her hair, and for a moment, she feared that he would not come. He might think it would be an insult to Jimmy, or that perhaps she would be angry with him. Then she resumed brushing her hair. Friedrich would come – if only to make sure she was all right. After that? He probably wouldn't come back until after Jimmy left. And by then he might be transferred to the canneries again for the winter months. This could be her last chance to see him.

She listened for sounds downstairs but heard only a few noises coming from the kitchen – the faucet running, a chair being moved, a few words exchanged as Jessica and Kate prepared breakfast. Sounds from the farmyard told her Jimmy was busy with chores. A gloom was beginning to settle on the house. There had been no word about Eugene.

Without it being alluded to, they were all beginning to think that if Eugene were alive, they would have heard something by now. He would have found a way to let them know. Their stories about why they hadn't heard anything were beginning to grow thin. Jessica suggested that maybe he had amnesia. Ursula thought perhaps he was in hiding. Jimmy was silent.

The strain of not knowing was beginning to show on their mother. Ursula had seen her, on more than one occasion, wandering around Eugene's room, looking through his clothes in the closet, smoothing down the quilt on his bed. Sometimes she would come upon her, lost in thought, staring out a window or down at the floor. The idea of a second son lost to the war surely filled her with a bottomless sorrow.

Ursula set the brush down, and wondered if her mother was haunted by the same terrible possibility, the fear that sometimes gripped her in the middle of the night: What if none of them came back?

"Ursula!" cried Jessica. "Breakfast is ready!"

*

In the late afternoon, as the sunlight slanted through the farmhouse windows, Kate made sure that Jessica and Jimmy were ready for the Bloomfield's Christmas party. She had begged off going, saying she didn't feel well; but they all understood that it was because of Eugene. She couldn't bear any more questions about him, or see any more expressions of pity.

She lit the burner to boil some water for a cup of tea, and sat down heavily on the kitchen chair while she waited.

Jimmy came into the kitchen. "Sure you don't want to go, Mom? I could run you back whenever you wanted."

Kate shook her head.

"Aw, come on, Mom," said Jimmy. "You'll enjoy yourself. Ursula will be all right on her own for a few hours."

Before Ursula could agree, Kate declined. "No. I'm feeling a bit under the weather. I'm looking forward to sitting on the couch and doing nothing. We'll listen to the radio. Go to bed early."

She smiled at Jimmy. "You look very handsome. And you, too, Jessica. What a shame Ursula can't go with you."

"She needs to nurse that hand of hers," said Jimmy. "The last thing she needs is someone banging into it."

"I'll make the tea, Mom," said Jessica. "Go rest on the couch."

Ursula walked into the living room with Kate, and turned on the radio, hoping to find some Christmas music. Jessica soon came in carrying two cups of tea.

Kate smiled her thanks, and curled up on the couch. She looked around for the quilt and then remembered that Jimmy had taken it upstairs.

"Jessica, before you go, bring me a quilt from the closet, will you?"

Jessica ran upstairs, followed by Ursula.

When Ursula reached the top of the stairs, Jessica was waiting for her. "Are you thinking what I'm thinking?" she whispered.

Ursula nodded. "We can still wrap it up for Christmas and put it under the tree. But it seems like the perfect time to give it to her. You bring it to her. She's still angry with me."

"No, she's not. She's just sad about – everything." Jessica ran to her room, folded up the quilt they had made, and gathered it in her arms. "Come."

Kate and Jimmy stopped their conversation when they saw Jessica and Ursula approach. "Goodness," said Kate with a smile. "What are you both so solemn about?"

Jimmy grinned. "You look like the Magi bearing gifts."

"We are," said Jessica, laughing. "We want to give you our Christmas present early, Mom. Is that all right? We'll wrap it up for Christmas if you want. But – it will keep you warm tonight. While you don't feel well."

Kate sat up on the couch. "Normally I would say no. No early presents. But you've got me curious. So yes, you may. What do you have there?"

Ursula nodded for Jessica to present the quilt.

"Ursula and I made it." She placed it on her mother's lap.

Kate unfolded it, and gasped on seeing the depiction of the farm. In a circle of beautifully embroidered vines and flowers – there was the farmhouse and garden, the pasture, the grove of maples and oaks, the old weeping willow.

"Jessica did the embroidery," said Ursula. "She's been working on it for months. Remember that drawing Aunt Lillian made when she was here? Jessica used that."

Kate sat speechless. She opened the quilt and spread it over the couch. There was her home. There was the farm that she and her husband had slaved over with so much love. There was the house, with the picket fence that Paul made. And the arbor! She looked up at Jimmy. "Did you see, Jimmy? The arch you made is here!"

An outer circle of embroidered words framed the picture: the names of everyone, special dates, key moments in their lives – all linked in an unending circle. Her sons and daughters, her husband. All of them. Forever linked. Kate's tears that had been building for so long, now brimmed and rolled down her cheeks. She clasped the quilt in her arms and buried her face in it.

Jessica dropped to her knees. "I'm sorry, Mom. We didn't think it would make you sad or we never would have given it."

Jimmy quietly left the room, and Ursula sat down next to her mother.

Kate wiped away her tears. "Not sad. So – happy." She gave a crooked smile and looked down at the quilt. "Our home! This makes me feel rich, and safe and secure. We have something that is so strong, that can never be taken away from us. Your father, Francy. Eugene. Are still here with us, are a part of us, forever."

She reached out for her daughters' hands. "It will keep me warm for many years to come." She started to examine the patchwork fabric. "Why, look here. That's Francy's shirt, isn't it? He loved that shirt and wore it till the elbows thinned out." She spotted another familiar pattern. "And that's my summer dress, the one your father loved so much." She looked up. "You mean you've been saving it all these years?"

Jessica nodded. "We've been talking about making this for years, haven't we Ursula?"

"Yes, and when Jessica burned the floral tablecloth with the iron, we finally had enough fabric."

"Probably did it on purpose," said Jimmy, who had come back into the room, now that the sadness had lifted.

"I did no such thing," laughed Jessica.

"All the same, don't you go near my clothes," he teased.

"Thank you, my girls. How did I get so lucky in my children?" She looked around at them.

"Now how am I going to top that?" asked Jimmy, steering them away from anything that might lead them all back to tears. "You girls always did outdo the rest of us."

"Oh, Jimmy, how can you say that?" Kate twisted the quilt to the embroidered house. "Look. There's the arbor you made that I always dreamed about. I'll plant it in roses this spring. Just you wait and see."

Jessica laughed. "Guess I'll have to embroider some roses. What color, Mom?"

"Red, I think," said Kate. "Red for love."

"Look at the time, Jess. We better get going. Gladys'll be waiting for us. Besides, I want to get there before Joe and Burly eat everything."

"No chance of that," said Jessica. "Shirley said Sue Ellen's been cooking all week." She kissed her mother goodbye. "Mrs. Bloomfield promised to pack a basket for you and Ursula. She knows how much you love her Christmas fudge and divinity."

Ursula draped her coat over her shoulders. "I'll just walk them to the truck, Mom. I could do with some fresh air."

It was four o'clock by the time they drove off. The day had grown dusky. A soft gray and rose sunset spanned the horizon. In the distance, she saw Ed and Otto leaning on the pasture fence; ahead of them the POWs were crossing to the other side of the pasture to call in the cows. But Friedrich wasn't with them. Her heart jumped. Here was her chance.

She stepped into the barn, and not seeing him there she went to the machine shed. She found him working on the generator.

He raised his head on seeing her enter. "They are gone?"

"Jimmy and Jessica have gone to the Bloomfield's. The others are down by the creek. Mom's inside."

He gently took her wrapped hand and inspected the discoloration, and winced at a few stitches that showed. "Oh, Ursula!"

"It's nothing. A little bruising."

He wrapped his arms around her. "I'm so sorry, Ursula. This is my fault. You were distracted, worried that – "

"No, Friedrich. I was careless."

He clasped her gently in his arms, careful of her hand.

"Your brother? He will make me leave the farm? Oh my God, the thought of losing you." He held her close and buried his face in her hair.

"He won't say or do anything," said Ursula. "I've asked him not to."

He placed his hand under her chin and raised her face to him, trying to read her face. "Have I lost you, Ursula?"

"How can you say that?" She looked more carefully at him, surprised at the desperation in his eyes. "Of course not."

"I have lost everything. But to think that I have lost you, too, Ursula, is more than I can bear. I hear what they say in town about – about you having someone in Peoria. I know it can't be true – and yet why does everyone believe it? And now, your brother will surely force me away from you."

"Friedrich," she said, taking his hand. "You know I love you."

He turned aside. "I think I know. But – I also know you are not being truthful with me." He gave a sad smile. "You are not a good liar, my Ursula."

She started to speak, but he held up his hand.

"I – I cannot be so selfish. You must do what makes you happy. That is what I want for you." Again, he raised his hand. "I know something is different. You don't want me to embrace you. Maybe it is because I struck your brother, and I am sorry for that. Or maybe your friend in Peoria is showing you another way that life can be."

He saw that she was trying to object to everything he said, but he was determined to have his say. "I want you to be happy. I will always love you, but I understand that our – that my love – that you must – " His voice broke and he couldn't go on.

Ursula cupped her hand against his cheek. "Friedrich, my love. I thought you knew me better than that."

He was afraid to hope, though he wanted to believe the truth in her eyes. "But then why? Why do you put a distance between us? I can feel it, here," he said, placing his fist over his heart.

"I didn't want to tell you yet…"

"Tell me what?" He braced himself for the blow. "Oh, my God, Ursula. The truth is better than not knowing. Please, tell me."

She looked at him lovingly, seeing the passion in his eyes, his mouth. She filled her gaze with the man she loved. Then she smiled tenderly. "Oh, Friedrich. Can't you guess?"

But she saw only desperate sadness is his eyes. She brought her face close to his, and kissed him. Then she took his hand, and gently placed it on her belly.

For one moment, his face still questioned her. He looked from her eyes, to their hands, then back to her lovely face. Then his eyes widened, and a short gasp escaped him. He took a step back to better see her. "You – you mean? You are – "

She laughed at his confusion and nodded.

Tears shot to his eyes. "Oh, my Ursula! My beautiful love." He kissed her mouth, her cheeks, her eyes, then he dropped to his knees and embraced her, placing his face softly against her belly and kissing it again and again.

She stroked his hair, and held him against her. "We will be a family, Friedrich."

He stood, and her heart melted to see the tears on his cheeks, the joy in his eyes.

He couldn't speak. He embraced her, and she felt the moment when he broke, and he sobbed into her hair. He wept for his new-found joy, and for the loss of those who would never share it with him.

"I had imagined so many reasons for your distance – but never this!" He kissed her again and again. "But how long – when – Are you all right? Have you seen a doctor?" He guided her to a bale of hay and gently had her sit, which caused her to laugh.

"I'm fine. I saw a doctor in Peoria. Twice. And that gave me the idea – that others might think I had a soldier there."

Friedrich put his head in his hands. "You fooled even me. I'm so sorry. To carry this burden alone." He suddenly looked up. "Oh, my God, Ursula. If anyone finds out! We must marry. I will find a way."

He jumped to his feet and began pacing. "I can't bring shame upon you. I must find a way. You must be able to say you are married. I couldn't bear it if anyone looked on you with scorn. Because of me."

"Yes, we must marry. But no one needs to know who the father is, who my husband is, for now."

"I hate any lie. And people will wonder, and ask – "

"But you would be taken away. We must keep it secret, Friedrich."

He shut his eyes and nodded. He finally sat next to her, his mind searching for a solution. "Listen, there's a priest from the same town as Karl. He will visit soon. I will tell you when. Perhaps – perhaps he would marry us."

"But how?"

He ran the impossibility through his mind, and his face fell. "I don't know. But I'll find a way."

Joy flooded her face at the glimmer of hope. This was more than she could have wished for. "Then I could say that I am married. No one would need to know anything more."

He kissed her and held her close, running his hand over her hair. "We will find a way. And when this war is over, we will be together." He stood again, and began pacing in hope, then sat down next to her, and kissed her again and again.

Then he gently took her left hand in his. "When I was over at the river, one day I walked with the foreman into a store. A little store that sold a mix of things. While I waited, I stood in front of a glass cabinet full of little boxes, watches, jewelry. Something sparkled in the sun and I stooped to see what it was. I saw a ring. It was amethyst – simple, but beautiful. Like these." He brushed her hair away to touch her earrings. "I wanted so badly to get it for you. My heart broke to think that I was not free to buy this ring for my beloved. But I knew then that one day, I would put an amethyst ring on your finger. As my wife."

"And you will, Friedrich. I will be your wife. However long it takes, we will be together. We will be waiting for you."

He clasped her in his arms. "I never thought I would be so happy again."

He stopped suddenly when he was seized with another thought. "Who – besides the doctor, who else knows?"

Ursula looked away. "Just one other person."

A shadow of worry filled his face. "Oh, my God. Your mother?"

Ursula shook her head.

"Jessica?"

Again, she shook her head.

They heard the others approaching with the cattle, and quickly separated. Ursula went to the side door, and briefly turned around. In answer to his questioning gaze, she answered softly. "Jimmy."

Chapter 13

∿

Lillian took off a few days to be with Charles. Though he was clearly still recovering, he soon felt well enough to go into the office. He was looking forward to seeing his old staff again.

Charles called her in the morning to say that Mrs. Sullivan and Mason insisted on taking him out for a welcome home dinner. "I'll be home a little late. You don't mind, do you?"

"Of course not! Enjoy your time. The boys will be delivering posters tonight with the Boy Scouts, so I think I'll ask Izzy to stop by. I promised Mr. Rockwell I would speak to her about coming back."

Lillian could hear the love in his voice as he told her he already missed her.

After Tommy and Gabriel came home from school, Lillian fixed them a quick dinner, and then helped them prepare for the Scouts meeting. She was just seeing them off when Izzy arrived. Lillian set out some olives, cheese, and crackers and poured them both a glass of wine.

Izzy sat down on the couch and admired the Christmas tree and decorations. "Christmas always looks better with kids around, doesn't it?" She raised her glass, took a sip, and eyed the plate of food. "So – I guess I know what this is all about."

Lillian smiled at Izzy's lack of enthusiasm. "I promised Mr. Rockwell that I would at least relay his message."

Izzy speared an olive and popped it into her mouth. "Well?"

"Well, the long and short of it is that he wants you back."

"Of course he wants me back," Izzy said. "Well, he's out of luck."

"On your terms."

Izzy's head snapped up. "He said that?" She leaned back and gave it some thought. "That doesn't sound like the Rockwell I know."

"He's tried a few of the girls, but gets utterly frustrated with them. He got used to you, Izzy, and the office just doesn't run smoothly without you." Lillian fixed a slice of cheese on a cracker and put it in her mouth, taking a moment to savor it. "There," she said, smiling. "I delivered his message. I told him I was one hundred percent sure you wouldn't be coming back and were perfectly happy at your new job. 'Where she is appreciated,' I added." Lillian leaned back and took a sip of wine.

When Izzy didn't say anything, Lillian set down her glass. "Izzy?"

Izzy cast a sideways glance at her.

"You wouldn't really consider going back, would you? Of course, I'd be thrilled, but I know how much you dislike Rockwell."

"True. But the job itself – I've always loved it. I never knew just how tedious examining records for gasoline fraud could be. I've never been so bored in my life."

"But there are other jobs, Izzy."

"Not many where I would have the degree of control I had at Rockwell. It took me years to get it, and it would take me years to earn at another place."

Lillian watched Izzy as she sat quietly, most likely running different scenarios through her mind.

"What exactly did he say? I mean the part about 'on my terms.'"

Lillian lifted and dropped her shoulders. "Those were his exact words. I don't know what he meant by them." After a moment's silence, she added, "Perhaps you should meet with him."

"I know Rockwell. He wouldn't have used those words unless he was desperate. I might be able to cut a deal." She took a sip of wine, and then gave a laugh. "I hate to admit it, but I miss the place. The whirlwind, the challenges every day, meeting with outside people, the expansion. I loved every minute of it." She let out a sigh. "But as he reminded me, it may very well come to an end anyway, when the war is over."

"Maybe you could convince him to keep you on. As part of a deal."

Izzy's eyes brightened. "A contract?"

"Well, I wasn't really thinking about anything specific – "

"That's brilliant, Lilly!" Izzy sat up, suddenly full of enthusiasm. "That's what's been missing."

"I guess you could at least try. If you don't like the terms, you won't have lost anything."

Izzy clinked her glass to Lillian's. "That's exactly what I'm going to do! I'll ask for the moon. I'll demand that Mr. Casey be rehired. With an increase in salary. And for me, a five-year contract. Maybe ten. While I'm asking, shall I try to get one for you, too?"

Lillian laughed at Izzy's exuberance. "Two weeks ago, I would have said, 'Absolutely!' But now…" She looked out, over her glass. "Meeting with Mrs. Huntington has clarified my thoughts. I realize now what I really want to do, how I want to work as an artist. She even spoke about a position."

Izzy raised her eyebrows at the news.

"I don't want to make any immediate changes," Lillian said. "I'll work on a freelance basis and see how it goes. She said there's definitely a market for my work. That's all I needed to hear."

"I understand. And this war will end. A freelance job would give you more time at home with Charles and the boys."

They exchanged a quick look, and for a moment Lillian was afraid Izzy would bring up the subject of having a baby. But Izzy knew of her disappointment, and kept quiet.

Izzy crunched on a cracker. "You won't leave anytime soon, will you? Now that I'm considering going back?"

Lillian laughed at the irony of the situation. "No. It's just an idea right now. I'll start working for Mrs. Huntington on the side, and get a better idea of the market and how it works. The next time I meet with her we'll discuss what sort of freelance arrangement will work best. I think in the long term, it would be good for me. It would give me more creative freedom."

"I'm happy for you, Lilly. You deserve it."

"I'll always be grateful to Mr. Rockwell for the opportunity he gave me, but – I don't see myself working there for much longer. Maybe in another year or so I'll put everything into working as a freelance agent."

"Maybe you'll be doing freelance work for Rockwell Publishing." Izzy gave a sly smile as she took another cracker with cheese. "If he hires me back, I'll have to work that into my new role. More say in the Art Department. Mr. Brache has some decidedly outdated ideas."

"What an improbable turn of events."

"Indeed." Izzy raised her glass again.

The two friends sat quietly for a few moments, each inside their own thoughts.

"You know, Izzy, Mr. Rockwell has been different lately."

"Different how?"

"He seems mellower, happier. He's been smiling more. You know how he never smiled."

"Jeez, I hope that's not the effect I have on people. I leave and they become happy."

"No, that's not it," said Lillian with a smile. "I think it might be because – well, twice now, you won't believe this – "

Izzy stopped mid sip. "What?"

"His wife – ex-wife, that is – has stopped by. And they went out to lunch together. The gossip is that he's been leaving work early and rushing out to meet her."

Izzy leaned back. "Well, well, well! That explains it! He's never gotten over her, you know. This could be good, Lilly. This could mean he would be there less, and not be breathing down my neck all the time. Maybe even delegate more of his responsibilities to me."

She squinted her eyes, playing out several possibilities, and then gave a big smile to Lillian. "From a strategic point of view, I think it's time to make my move!"

"I have to say this is not the conversation I thought we would be having. But I'm delighted!"

"Yes – you leaving Rockwell Publishing, and me going back."

Just then the door opened, and Charles walked in, his energy still high from the dinner. Lillian jumped up to greet him, and Izzy had to smile at the couple, so obviously in love.

Izzy got up to leave but Charles and Lillian persuaded her to stay and have a drink together, to catch up.

As Charles settled in, Lillian told him about Izzy's possible return to Rockwell Publishing.

"It's funny how you become attached to the place you work," said Lillian. "Even when conditions are not ideal."

"That's an understatement," Izzy said. "But I do love the job, the work, and, except for Rockwell, the people." She leaned her head to one side in consideration. "And even Rockwell has his good points."

"What about you, Charles?" Lillian asked. "How did it feel to be back at the firm after being gone for so long?"

"I never knew how much I missed the old place. Mrs. Sullivan, Mason, Edith. I told Edith I just missed seeing Desmond in London, by a day or so. But here's some news you'll both find interesting." He set his glass down and leaned forward. "You'll never guess who I saw in London."

Lillian and Izzy exchanged looks. "Tell us!" said Lillian.

"Mr. Weeble."

Izzy choked on her drink. "No!"

"*Our* Mr. Weeble?" asked Lillian.

"The very same. I was introduced to him at the War Office and when I recognized the name, I asked him where he was from. And I realized that he was your nemesis-turned-advocate. He sends his regards. I gather he's with Intelligence."

"Good Lord!" said Izzy. "Will wonders never cease – Rockwell's old office manager in Intelligence?"

Charles got up to open another bottle of wine. From the kitchen he continued the conversation. "And I bumped into Red a few times. You know he's back in London after being stationed at Polebrook. He always asks about you, Izzy. I told him what I knew from Lillian's letters. He's doing much better from the last time I saw him." He sat back down and poured them all another glass.

"You mean – his leg wound?" Izzy asked quietly.

Charles leaned back and considered how to answer her question. "No, it's more like his mental state. Less dejected than a year ago. No, I'd say his health is quite good now. Has a bit of a limp is all. Though I think his vision still causes him problems."

Izzy took a sip of wine. "And did you – did you meet his wife?"

Charles looked up in surprise. "His wife? No. That was over about as soon as it began. A month." He leaned back and took a sip of wine. "Maybe two."

He suddenly became aware that the room had grown quiet. He gave a quick glance to Lillian who was staring into her wine glass. Izzy had gone pale.

"Oh – I – I'm so sorry. I assumed you knew. I thought Lillian would have told you."

"I would have, had I known," Lillian replied, with an edge to her voice. "You never told me this, Charles."

"I'm sure I wrote to you about it at the time."

Izzy rose to her feet. "I don't know if it's the wine, or if this evening has been just too full of information for my poor head, but I feel positively dizzy." She gave a laugh, and put her hand on

Lillian's arm. "Time I went home. I have to prepare for my battle with Rockwell."

Lillian saw that Izzy was trying her best to appear cheerful, but was completely unsettled by the news about Red.

Izzy put on her coat and hat. "I'll tell you all about it. Good seeing you, Charles!" she said, closing the door behind her.

The blood rose to Lillian's face and she began to clear away the dishes. "How could you have spoken so casually to her about Red!"

Charles was taken aback. "I thought she knew. Besides, you told me it was all over between them."

"Something like that can never be over! They were engaged to be married." She put the dishes in the sink with a bang. "Red was the love of her life. She's never loved anyone else."

Charles stood at the couch. "Well – How was I supposed to know that?"

"And then he turned around and married his nurse? I hope you could never so easily forget me." She waved her hand in the air, and then brought the glasses to the sink. "If you were to meet a younger woman who you could still have children with!"

"What are you talking about?" he said, following her into the kitchen. "Red didn't say anything about children or – Where is all this coming from, Lillian?"

His question was met with silence. He walked up behind her as she was rinsing the dishes.

"Don't tell me this is still about our argument in the spring. I thought this time was going to be different."

She turned off the water, and looked down at the dishes. "So did I."

"I promised myself that nothing was going to get in our way this time."

Lillian dried her hands and set the towel down. "So did I."

Charles placed his hands on her shoulders and turned her around. When she kept her eyes cast down, he lifted her face and tried to read her expression. "What are you so upset about? I told you I have more than I ever could have hoped for with you and the boys." He pulled out a kitchen chair and sat down on it, and then pulled her onto his lap. "Don't you believe me?"

She took a deep breath and let it out, as if in defeat. "I just wanted to hear you say that it wasn't too late. That I wasn't too old to have another child. I thought if *you* believed it, then it would be true. I could still hope." Her eyes filled with vulnerability. "After we argued, I waited and waited for you to say something, but you became more distant instead. I was so hurt, Charles."

"Wait a minute, that's not – Now I'm completely confused." He cocked his head as if seeing once again their argument in the spring. "I have never said anything about your age. How could I? *You* were the one who complained about *my* age."

Lillian's eyes widened in anger. "I did no such thing!"

"Yes, you did. You said age most likely played a role. And I *am* ten years older than you. What other conclusion could I come to?"

Lillian jumped to her feet. "I didn't mean you! I meant me!"

Now Charles rose to his feet. "Well, you sure didn't say that!"

"That's absurd. Men can have children until they're a hundred years old!" She folded her arms. "So that's why you thought I had some young man in my life. I knew what you were getting at about Henry, don't pretend you didn't."

They looked at each other in a stand-off – and then realizing the absurdity of the argument, they burst out laughing.

"So, we just spent half a year thinking we were too old for each other?" asked Lillian.

Charles pulled her towards him. "You will never be old to me. Never." He squeezed her in an embrace, and buried his face in her neck. "One hundred? Really?"

And they fell into helpless laughter.

Tommy and Gabriel rushed into the apartment just at that moment, and their mouths dropped open to see their parents laughing so hard that tears were coming from their eyes.

"What?" asked Tommy.

"Tell us!" said Gabriel, who like Tommy, was starting to laugh along with them.

"Your mother – " began Charles.

"No! Your father – " but Lillian couldn't finish, and fell into Charles.

Gabriel turned to Tommy and shrugged. "Mom said Dad says some very funny things sometimes," which caused Lillian to laugh all the harder.

Chapter 14

Ursula read at the kitchen table, waiting for Jimmy to come home. He was spending more and more time with Gladys; today he had spent nearly the whole day with her. Ursula had gotten up several times, thinking she heard the pickup truck turn into the lane. Each time she returned to her book, and waited. She had spoken to Friedrich briefly that afternoon about a plan, and now she was desperate for Jimmy's help.

An hour later, she finally heard the truck drive up the lane and pull into the farmyard.

Jimmy came in, surprised to see her sitting at the kitchen table. He hung up his jacket and rubbed his hands. "Cold out there! What are you doing still up?"

"Just reading. I heated up some milk. Can I make you some hot cocoa?"

He shook his head.

"How was the movie?"

"Fine, if you like movies where they sing about everything. Gladys liked it." He pulled off his boots and set them by the door. "I didn't like the newsreels. It's getting worse and worse in Belgium, the Netherlands – terrible cold. People are freezing and starving to death."

He plopped down on a chair. "Goddamn Germans," he muttered.

Now was not the right time to ask for his help – but the priest would arrive tomorrow. She had to ask Jimmy tonight.

He stretched out his legs, and told her about the people he had seen in town. Then he absent-mindedly began humming the melody from the movie *Meet Me in St. Louis*, and frowned. "It was one of those happy stories where everything works out in the end. Things got better after the movie."

He clearly wasn't in the right frame of mind, but desperation urged her on. She went to the hall and saw that her mother's bedroom door was closed, and then came back to the table.

"I need to talk to you, Jimmy. I need your help with something."

"So, that's why you're still up. I don't like the sound of this."

"I need you to drive me to town tomorrow evening."

"Can I ask why?"

Ursula studied the table, then answered. "It's better if you don't know."

He pushed his chair back. "I can't risk getting into any trouble."

"I know. That's why I won't tell you anything. I just need a ride into town. I can't drive with this hand or I would drive myself in."

Jimmy started to hum the melody again, and put his hands behind his head. "There was a feature on buying war bonds, and a cartoon – "

"Jimmy. This is serious."

"We'll see. But it's starting to snow. Could be heavy."

His dismissive attitude worried Ursula. "I must go into town tomorrow. I just need you to cover for me." She waited for him to respond. Finally, he looked up.

"I'm not going to agree to something blindly. You have to let me know what I'm getting involved in."

Ursula leaned in closer and spoke in a low voice. "There's a priest from the same town as Karl who will visit the camp tomorrow. Friedrich met him once before. A kind man. He might be able to help us."

"Marry you?" Jimmy scoffed. "In the camp? You're really grabbing at straws."

"Shhh! Lower your voice." She went to the hall again to listen, and then sat back down. "I don't know how it will work. But it's the only chance we have."

"You're just going to waltz into the camp and – "

"I'll say I'm there to apply for a job at the canteen. They're always looking for help. Or maybe Friedrich can find a way to get out. All we need is a few minutes. We have to at least try."

"That's the most hare-brained idea I've ever heard of."

"But it's the only chance we have! Will you do it? You can take Gladys out and just drop me off – "

They heard a door open and footsteps coming down the hall. "Jimmy, is that you?" Kate came into the kitchen, and rubbed her arms. "Ursula! You're still up? It's freezing in here." She saw the pan of milk on the stove. "Just what I had in mind."

Ursula glanced at Jimmy and hoped he wouldn't say anything. It must have been the newsreel that put him in this mood. She wished she had not spoken to him.

Kate went to the stove and touched the side of the pan. "Still hot." She turned to Jimmy. "Are you hungry? Did you have anything to eat?"

"Did I ever. Gladys fed me till I was ready to burst. She's some cook, I can tell you that. Then after the movie we went to the Wulrich farm and played cards. And ate some more."

Kate looked from Jimmy to Ursula, noticing the coldness between them. "And what were you two talking about?"

"Weddings," said Jimmy.

Ursula flushed at the word and shot a look of warning to Jimmy.

"Weddings?" Kate asked, clearly amused. She stirred the milk and then filled a cup. "Don't tell me you're getting serious about Gladys?"

"She's a pretty nice girl. She's dutiful. Patriotic."

Ursula's color deepened at the oblique insults.

"Strange praise," said Kate. She opened the jar of honey and added some to her cup. "She's also very pretty and has been interested in you for a long time."

"Oh, yeah. That too. So, I'm going to take her into town tomorrow, if the snow stops. Take her out to dinner. You want to come along, Ursula?"

"Well, that's not very romantic, Jimmy," said Kate.

"Exactly," he said. "For the time being, I don't want her getting any ideas."

Kate laughed and took a sip. "How about some hot milk with honey?"

He shook his head. "It doesn't mix with beer very well. But maybe a cup would be good for Ursula."

Ursula shook her head. "I – I already had some."

Kate took her cup of milk and started to leave. "Don't stay up too late." She patted Jimmy's shoulder. "You too, Ursula."

Ursula nodded. "Goodnight, Mom."

They heard her go back down the hall, into her room, and close her door. Jimmy pushed off from the table. "It's a crazy, mixed up world. That's all I have to say." He left the kitchen, and went upstairs.

*

Overnight, the snow continued to fall, blanketing the fields and roads. In the morning, Ursula stood at the kitchen window, disheartened by the whiteness outside. It was already over a foot deep and falling heavily.

As she and her mother prepared breakfast, Ed called to say that the camp wouldn't be sending the prisoners today due to the snow. "Looks like we'll be getting a lot of it. It's one of those days, best to just hunker down and give in to nature."

Jimmy had woken early to feed and water the animals. He came inside the back porch, stomped the snow off his boots, and shook the snow from his jacket before hanging it up. He entered the kitchen, avoiding Ursula's worried eyes. "It's coming down hard," he said.

"No school for me. Here," said Jessica, pouring him a cup of coffee, and then sitting down beside him. "You'll have to cancel your plans with Gladys for today. Looks like you're stuck with us."

"It'll pass," said Ursula, pulling aside the curtain. "The sky's already getting lighter."

"Which sky are you talking about?" asked Jimmy. "It's not letting up any time soon. No one's getting in or out of town today." He smiled at the plate of biscuits and gravy Kate set in front of him.

"It's a good day for you to stay inside and just relax," Kate said. "I'll make you a nice meal for supper."

Like Jessica, Kate was delighted by the snow, for it meant more time with Jimmy.

Though he used much of the day to fix things around the house, Jessica spent almost every minute with him, appointing herself his assistant, and later forced him into a game of checkers. And Kate was filled with utter contentment when he sat at the kitchen table and talked to her while she baked a pie and then prepared dinner.

Throughout the day, whenever she found a chance, Ursula tried to convince Jimmy that the snow was letting up and they could get into town. Each time it ended with them quarreling over it.

"I'm not going to get stuck in a ditch because of some hare-brained idea of yours."

"But Jimmy – "

"I said no!"

In the afternoon, Jimmy saw that she had shoveled part of the porch and was starting to clear the steps.

He snatched the shovel away from her. "Damn it, Ursula, leave it alone! You're not supposed to be using that hand. Get inside." He continued with the shoveling, but didn't relent on his decision.

The snow did taper off by evening, but the roads wouldn't be clear anytime soon. Ursula was overcome with a sense of defeat. She and Friedrich had missed their only opportunity. The priest was there for only a day.

Ursula was quiet over dinner, and went upstairs early. She took a hot bath and let her tears fall. Then she took a book and crawled into bed, propping up the pillows behind her. From downstairs, she could hear laughter from Jessica and Jimmy as they listened to the *Fibber McGee and Molly* show on the radio. Ursula set the book down and gazed out at nothing. She was all alone in this. She would have to live with her predicament – her life a secret, shutting down to the outside world.

And yet, she didn't regret it. Not one minute of it. Her soul hungered for Friedrich and nothing would ever change that. She remembered the end-of-summer sweetness, the magical moonlit swim. They had arranged to meet at the pond; Friedrich had risked leaving the camp at night so that they could be alone together. From the dock they had eased themselves into the cool, spring-fed water, the surface still warm from the heat of the day. They swam in an unearthly beauty, body to body, earth force coursing through them and the night. If she closed her eyes, she could still see his wet shoulder in the moonlight, gleaming gold. Nothing would ever compare to that moonlit night. She was sure that's when she had conceived. A child of moonlight and love. What could be more perfect? No, there was no regret. She would just have to wait for this terrible war to be over. Even it took long years... She was startled by a knock at her door.

"Yes?" She leaned forward.

Jimmy poked his head inside. "Mom's asking if you want a cup of tea. She's afraid you're coming down with something." He heard his words and chuckled. "That's an understatement."

Ursula grew angry at the lightness of his tone. "We could have tried to get to town. We've driven in snow before." She lifted her book, and made a pretense of reading.

"Not in this kind of snow. We would have gotten stuck, and then what? March you through the snow? In your condition?"

Ursula didn't look up.

"You're just being stubborn," he said. Then he noticed the shadows under her eyes, and spoke more gently. "Look. If we couldn't get into town, then neither could that priest. Use your head, Ursula."

"We could have tried."

He lost his temper at her unreasonableness. "Why do you always have to be so impulsive about everything? That's always been your problem. Headstrong. Your way. And look where it's got you."

Her mouth was quivering but her sudden sob took him by surprise. "Don't, Jimmy. I can't bear for you to be like this to me, to think so low of me."

"Don't be so goddamned desperate. I'm just – Aw, hell, it's just the way of the world. It's not your fault. Nothing's easy. It might take some time, but it'll all work out."

Ursula lifted the quilt to her tears.

Jimmy glanced down the hallway, and then rubbed his foot on the wooden floor, keeping his eyes on the doorknob. "Look. I'm only going to say this once. I don't approve. Not a bit. But there's one thing I'm sure of. He loves you. If he didn't, I'd have to hurt him. Chances are he's just a regular guy who got caught up in the war. Like me. Like all of us."

Ursula raised her eyes.

"When you hurt your hand, he was frantic. He's a good man. I can see that." He saw that her mouth was trembling, and he shifted back to anger, that ground being much firmer to stand on. "But you have a rough road ahead of you, and you're going to have to face what you've done."

"I know that! You don't need to remind me of it."

"Well, if you ask for my help, then you better expect a little advice!"

Suddenly, Jessica was standing in the doorway. "I brought you a cup of tea."

They both looked at her, wondering how much she had heard.

Jessica set the cup on the bedside table and directed her words to Jimmy. "Why have you two been so quarrelsome today? You should stop it. Mom notices it and it makes her sad."

"God dang, two bossy sisters! Little sisters! I can't wait to be back on ship." And he left the room and went downstairs.

Jessica remained looking at Ursula.

"We weren't arguing, Jessica. Just – disagreeing about something."

Jessica went to the door and closed it, and then smiled. "He's never as angry as he pretends to be. He's got a big ole soft heart that he's always trying to hide." She walked to the bed and sat down on the edge.

Ursula looked at her with questioning eyes.

"Are you all right, Ursula?"

"I'm fine. I'm just tired." Ursula picked up her book, uncomfortable with Jessica's piercing gaze. She waited for her to leave the room and go back downstairs, but Jessica remained sitting on the bed, tracing her finger over a flower in the quilt.

After a few moments of silence, Jessica spoke softly. "Ursula. I know."

Ursula's head popped up, and she fixed her sister with an angry stare. "Know what?"

Jessica tilted her head to the side as if to say, *I'm not a baby anymore.* "And I know that Jimmy knows. I overheard you two the other night."

Ursula felt her heart pounding. She had often found Jessica watching her, and knew she had overheard the argument with Jimmy – but surely she didn't know what they were arguing about. She couldn't know! Ursula remained silent, hoping that Jessica had misunderstood.

"I've suspected it for a while," Jessica continued. "You had me fooled with the whole Peoria thing. Then I finally figured it out when we learned that Dolores was up in Seneca. I'm glad it's Friedrich – "

"Jessica!" Ursula leaned forward and grabbed her sister's arm. "Stop! Don't say another word. You mustn't say another word." She eyed the closed door. "It could be treason! We could lose the farm. I don't know what they would do to him. But they would surely take him away from me. And I couldn't bear it."

Ursula buried her face in her hands and tried not to give in to her tears.

Jessica looked on in alarm at her strong sister who never cried, who never let anything frighten her.

"Don't worry, I won't say anything. But I thought you might like to know – I'm on your side. And I know Jimmy knows and was trying to help. Though I'm still in shock over that."

"Oh, my God! Jessica – listen to me. Never say anything more about Jimmy! He could be court-martialed. Or worse! I *never* meant for him to know. Or you. You shouldn't know any of this."

"It's not as if you can hide it," said Jessica, ever practical. "Besides, everyone already thinks you met someone in Peoria. And I told a little white lie to Shirley that Sue Ellen just happened to over-hear. About a letter you dropped that I happened to pick up, full of mushy language. From a certain Corporal who's temporarily stationed at Camp Ellis and has friends in Peoria."

Ursula looked at her sister with incredulity, and then impulsively embraced her. She didn't want anyone else involved. And yet an enormous burden was lifted. At least in front of Jessica, she no longer had to pretend. And knowing that her sister was on her side made her feel stronger. Jimmy, and now Jessica. It would make the rest easier.

"How did you know?"

Jessica made a small sound of disbelief. "Throwing up in the mornings, gaining weight, looking worried as hell."

Ursula suddenly pieced together something that had been bothering her, sitting at the back of her mind, not quite making sense. Several times, when someone had mentioned Ursula's weight gain, or baggy clothes, Jessica had explained it away, also taking to wearing loose clothing and saying she too was gaining weight, though she wasn't. Ursula's heart melted; her wise little sister had been protecting her all along. She gave a sad smile.

"You've been covering for me."

Jessica answered with a light shrug.

"How long have you known? I thought I was being so careful. Do you think anyone else suspects?"

"I've seen Ed watching you two. But I don't think he knows how serious it is. For a long time I didn't know. I thought you hated him. Then I started to notice little things, but I thought you were just being nicer to them all. But then in August – "

"What?"

Jessica looked away. "Do you remember the milkweed outing I was in charge of?"

Ursula nodded, and quickly scanned her memory. "But you were all gathering in the south field. We weren't even in the same area that day. I made sure of it."

"It was before that, when I was scouting out locations. I was following the fence north of the creek. And I saw you. Both of you. Kissing. That's when I knew."

Ursula knew exactly which day she meant. She had ridden her bike out to the north pasture, knowing that Friedrich was there alone. She had brought him lunch. And they had spent two heavenly hours together, alone. She had spread the tablecloth and pretended that they were just an ordinary couple, courting, having a picnic.

Ursula dropped her face into her hands. She had been careless. She had risked too much over the summer. She laid her hand on Jessica's shoulder. "Jessica, listen to me. You must *never* speak of this again. I mean – about Friedrich. Please. Pretend you don't know. At least until the war is over. Can you do that?"

"Of course. I've done it this long, haven't I?"

"Mom will realize soon enough. About this," Ursula said, placing her hand on her belly. "If it weren't for the worry about Eugene, I'm sure she would have noticed. I want to wait until after Jimmy goes to tell her. After Christmas. But she mustn't know about Friedrich. She would have to do something about it."

Ursula tried to imagine what lay ahead, and as always, all she saw was difficulty and scorn. And an ever-widening chasm between her and her mother that deeply saddened her. "I hope one day she can forgive me."

Jessica stood and smiled. "Ursula, what's done is done. Don't fret over it more than you have to. Like Ed always says, 'It'll all work out in the end.' And he's always been right." She started to leave, but added. "And don't worry. I won't let Jimmy know that I know."

Ursula watched her little sister, always level-headed and loving, leave the room. With her hand on the doorknob, Jessica turned to give a smile, and then closed the door.

Chapter 15

~

Over dinner, the excitement grew in Tommy and Gabriel as they told Charles all the things they would show him when they went upstate.

"Remember, boys, we won't have time to do everything we did last year," explained Lillian. "We'll only be there for a week this time."

"That still gives us plenty of time," said Gabriel. "We'll show you the beaver dam, and we know of an old logging road we can hike."

"And if it snows, Uncle Bernie will give us a sleigh ride. Last year we took a ride at night."

Lillian was delighted to be going to her sister's for Christmas. A week up at the orchard, away from everything, would be good for them all. And when they returned, they would have their anniversary celebration. She wanted to make it memorable, even if they decided to stay at home.

Over dessert, Tommy and Gabriel were just starting to tell Charles about the bonfire they built, when the telephone rang, causing an interruption to their story.

Lillian and Charles exchanged a look, and then Lillian went to the living room and answered the phone.

Her face fell. "It's for you," she said, handing the receiver to Charles.

He took the call. They all watched him listen in silence. His eyes darted quickly to Lillian, and she saw a glimmer of fear. Then he agreed to something, and they overheard his words: "I'll leave first thing in the morning."

He hung up the receiver, but kept his face turned away for a few moments, not wanting to see their disappointment.

Lillian placed her hand on his arm. "Charles?"

"I have to report to headquarters tomorrow."

Lillian asked with her eyes what it meant; she was sure it was bad news.

"The Germans have broken through our lines. They've launched a counter-attack."

"But – that's impossible! We've been pushing them back for months. How? Where?"

"They've broken through the Western Front in Belgium. The Ardennes Forest, thought to be impenetrable for a large-scale military operation." Charles shook his head, not quite believing that tanks had gotten through, and knowing that the lines would be thinnest there. "A blitzkrieg. They took us by surprise. And the weather is against us. Our planes can't fly."

"Do they have a chance?" Lillian whispered.

Charles's eyes narrowed. "They'll try to retake Antwerp, and cut off our supplies." He stared out at the vision in his mind. "They're desperate. They'll give it their all."

"Oh, my God. Will it never end?" Lillian leaned her head against his chest.

Charles saw that Tommy and Gabriel were watching. He put on a smile and returned to the table. "Sorry, boys. I'm afraid I have to leave tomorrow for a meeting. Most likely for a few days."

"But you'll be back, right?" asked Tommy.

"They already promised you could be with us for Christmas," said Gabriel. "They can't change their minds now."

"It looks like I'll be returning in a few days to fly out of New York. So, we might be able to have an early Christmas, before I leave. I'll know more after tomorrow."

"But – that means you won't be able to go to Aunt Annette and Uncle Bernie's," said Gabriel.

Lillian sat in stunned disbelief. She waved her hand in the direction of the radio. "I heard just yesterday that there was already talk about the peacetime conversion! I just can't believe it." Then she saw that tears were rolling down Gabriel's cheeks and dropping in his potatoes. But no words of comfort came to her.

Tommy looked around at the dismal faces. "Come on, Gabe. We have to be tough. Dad might get to come back before he goes." He looked up from one parent to the other. "They can't still win, can they? This is just a last-ditch effort? Right, Dad?"

Charles nodded. "I believe so."

Gabriel looked up at Lillian and spoke in a shaky voice. "Can I give Dad his present in case he misses Christmas?"

"Of course, you can. After dinner we'll have an early Christmas celebration." Lillian had tried to sound cheerful, but in the middle of speaking, her voice broke. She took a few dishes to the sink and began rinsing them.

*

Charles lay awake in the middle of the night, his mind teeming with thoughts and images. Not wanting to wake Lillian, he got out of bed and went to the living room. He sat on the couch in the dark. That he would be going back so soon jarred his mind. He had been so sure the war with Germany would be over in a few months. He thought of the servicemen, some recently arrived, others exhausted from years of fighting. They had most likely been unprepared, their minds on Christmas, on better times ahead. He imagined the frenzied activity as they scrambled to defend themselves, the loss of lives. A low moan escaped him.

Who knew how long it would last? What if the rumors were true that Germany had a secret weapon? He hated to admit it, but he didn't want to go back. There were too many bad memories, too much he had seen. He had no stomach for any of it anymore.

He rubbed his face, and looked up at the dark ceiling. He hungered for openness, for a clear sky, not one full of smoke, not one where he never knew if he was looking at stars or enemy planes. Would he ever look upon a sky of purity again?

"Charles?" Lillian asked, coming into the room. She waited a moment, and then sat next to him.

"Couldn't sleep," he said in a matter-of-fact tone, nothing to worry about.

But Lillian was worried. She had noticed a new habit in Charles this time. He would stare out at nothing, as if in disbelief, as if whatever his mind saw could not possibly be true, and then rub his face, rubbing away the vision. The weariness in him hurt her.

She plugged in the Christmas tree lights, and their softness helped to dispel the darkness.

She curled up next to him and wrapped her arm around his neck. "Charles. You never speak about it, but it must be terrible. Is there anything you want to talk about?"

The hellish images swirled together: the senseless death of Michael and so many others; the stench of human flesh when a ship was torpedoed; the men who were trapped in the sinking ships; the cries of agony and pain that surrounded him in the hospital…

"Charles." She gently placed her hand on his cheek. "Wouldn't it help for me to carry some of the burden?"

He buried a kiss in her hand. "No. I don't want what's in here," he touched his head, "to get into here," he stroked her hair. "I need to know that this place I come to," he kissed her head, "is unsullied by all that."

"Can't I take away some of the sadness in you? Some of the awfulness of war? Wouldn't it help to talk about it?"

"Maybe someday. But for now, your love is all that matters. It alone makes everything else fade away." He beheld his source of all solace and hope. So beautiful, so pure. She was his remedy against world-weariness, against despair.

She held him tightly. "Charles, I'm sorry I added to your pain. I should have told you straight away about Henry. I knew what you were thinking."

"It's not that, Lillian."

"And what I said about having a baby – I don't need it, Charles. I just thought it was something you would like. All I care about is that you're safe."

He took her hand and brought it to his lips. "You mean everything in the world to me. I could never ask for more."

He would go back, he had to go back. To protect everything she and the boys represented. There wasn't room for weariness and dread and fear. This was the time for every man to muster the last of his strength, the last of his reserves – and push on to defeat the enemy. The love and protection he felt for Lillian made him stalwart in his resolve.

*

It was with a heavy heart that Lillian saw Charles off in the early morning. Every goodbye was laced with the fear that it might be the last. She went to work and got through the day by keeping busy, grateful for the distraction of meetings and her work load.

When she left at end of day, she was surprised to find Izzy waiting for her in the hallway.

"Izzy! What are you doing here?"

"Just had my meeting with Rockwell, and thought I'd stop by to see if you were in – though I really didn't expect to find you." She immediately saw the worry in Lillian's eyes. "Not bad news, I hope?"

"Charles had orders to return to headquarters. He'll call tonight to let me know what it means for him. So, I thought I'd come in and catch up on a few things."

Izzy groaned. "I heard about it on the radio this morning. Couldn't believe it. We've had them on the run for months."

They left the building discussing the turn of events.

"I really thought it would be over soon," said Lillian. "In Europe. And I let myself hope that just maybe Charles wouldn't have to go to the Pacific. Now I'm beginning to wonder if it will ever end. How long can people stand it?"

"It'll end all right, Lilly. Our boys'll make sure of that." She placed her hand on Lillian's arm. "Oh, I hope it doesn't mean he'll miss Christmas with you. And your anniversary."

Lillian brushed the idea away, as if those things didn't matter in the scope of things. "I'll know more tonight." She couldn't bear to think of it. "Tell me how your meeting with Rockwell went."

Izzy thrust her hands in her pockets and a glint of triumph shone from her face. "He wants me in tomorrow."

Lillian couldn't hide her surprise. "So, it went well?"

"It was a bit contentious at first, but we were both bluffing. In the end, I got a raise, a contract, and he agreed to give Mr. Casey his job back – with a contract. Of course, now Rockwell can work me even harder. But to tell the truth, I can't wait to get started. It'll keep my mind off other things."

Lillian turned to look at her. "You mean – "

Izzy nodded. "I can't stop thinking about Red."

"I'm so sorry, Izzy. I know that was a shock for you to hear. All this time. In his cards at Christmas he always asked about you, but never once did he mention the divorce."

"I've been thinking about it all – how we met, our time together, our engagement and how happy we were." She shook her head. "He so wanted to do his part. Not waiting for the U.S. to enter the war, but going to Canada and joining there. Then his injury. He must have been so dejected. And then marrying his nurse. He reached out to me in a few cards and letters, and I ignored him." She squeezed her eyes shut. "I behaved badly, Lilly. I was so wrapped up in my own pain, I never thought about his. It's hard to imagine what goes on – over there. He reached out to me, and I turned away."

Lillian saw the regret in her eyes. "Does it change anything?"

Izzy gave a short laugh. "I've never been one to forgive anything that smacks of betrayal. I was so angry. And hurt. And so sure I could never forgive him. But in the bits and pieces of information I did read in his cards, and from what I've heard other GIs say, I think it may have been something else. What they call battle fatigue – confusion, depression, disorientation, desperation. Several of his crew had been killed; one of them died in his arms. Red was wounded – God knows what state of mind he was in. I – I never answered any of his letters. We were friends, too. And I let him down. He needed me and I was too proud to bend, to offer my help."

They walked in silence for a while, and then stopped.

"What will you do? Will you write to him?"

Izzy shrugged. "I suppose I will, though God knows what I'll say. I want him to know that I still hold him dear. But things have changed. We can never go back, can we?"

"No. The war has changed all that. None of us can go back to what we were. But I think we now value friendship and love more than ever. Don't you think?"

Izzy slowly nodded. "I suppose so." Then she took Lillian's arm and picked up their pace. "Come on," she said brightly. "I know you want to get home to wait for Charles's call."

When they parted ways at the corner, Lillian called out to her friend. "Izzy! Are we on for lunch tomorrow?"

Izzy spun around. "You bet we are!"

Chapter 16

Though it was just a few days before Christmas, Jimmy was frequently gone. He was making trips to nearby towns for some Christmas shopping, hoping to find something special for Gladys. Ursula felt a pang of sorrow that he had so easily forgotten her predicament, or chose to ignore it. She couldn't blame him. He only had another ten days before he had to leave. And yet she was glad that no more was spoken about her situation. She could not involve Jimmy and Jessica; it was far too risky for them. She would keep it to herself and deal with it.

Ursula helped her mother with the pies for the dinner that took place before the Christmas dance in town. Kate usually enjoyed the preparations, but this year her heart wasn't in it. And Ursula understood why. The night before, Ursula had gotten out of bed, wondering at the sound down the hall. She found her mother in Eugene's room, touching the chest of drawers, the pillows on his bed, his books on the side table. Ursula had heard her whisper the words, "My boy." Ursula had crept back to bed, her heart broken. To lose a brother had been shattering. But to lose a child – was there any greater pain?

Jessica was thrilled that the day of the big Christmas dance had finally arrived. She spent all morning deciding between two dresses and how to wear her hair. Then she flitted about the house in last minute preparations.

Ursula didn't want to go to the dance, but Kate and Jimmy kept pressing her. She couldn't use her hand as an excuse any longer. She had stopped using the sling a week ago, and the stitches would come out soon. Not only was she in no mood for merriment, but she didn't want to leave her mother alone.

Kate kept up a cheerful front. "You must go, Ursula! Please, it'll make me happy for you all to go together. Jimmy won't be here much longer. I'd like to see all of you dressed up and going to the dance."

Jimmy exaggerated his sulkiness, throwing his hands in the air. "I can't believe it! I come all the way home and my own sister won't help me celebrate. Why don't you go, too, Mom? Maybe she'd go if you would."

"Oh, I don't feel up to it. I'm still fighting this – cold, or whatever. But I really wish you would go, Ursula. You'll do it for me, won't you?"

Ursula nodded and smiled. How could she say no?

"Hold this side down, will you?" Jessica asked Ursula, handing her one end of the canvas banner she was adding a final touch to. She spread it across the kitchen table.

"And Jimmy, I need you to hold this side. I just have to add an arrow here."

Kate looked on her three children and smiled. She went to the row of hooks and reached for her jacket. "I think I'll get some air. Check the mail." She saw that Jimmy started to release his side. "Don't stop what you're doing. I'll be right back," she said, closing the door behind her.

Jimmy exchanged a look with his sisters.

"Oh, let her, Jimmy," said Jessica. "It helps her to keep busy. Hold it taut now!" She carefully painted in the arrow she had earlier traced.

"Like people need to be told which direction the entrance is," scoffed Jimmy, growing impatient. "The line will be a mile long!"

Jessica frowned at his remark. "Last year everyone tried to come in the side door. Anyway, this was Shirley's idea and I told her I would do it. There. Finished." She weighted down the sides with a few books, so the paint wouldn't pucker the canvas. She took a step back and nodded at the result.

Ursula moved to the window, and watched her mother. She saw her at the end of the lane, where she opened the mailbox and gathered the mail. Kate searched through the letters – and then froze. She held one letter out in front of her.

Ursula moved the curtain aside, and softly gasped.

"What is it, Ursula?" Jessica asked.

Jimmy and Jessica came and stood next to her. They saw that Kate stood, as if in indecision, staring at a letter in her hand.

"Oh, no," said Jessica, kneading her hands together.

Kate stood immobile. Then she turned the letter over. Still she hesitated. And then she began to open it.

Ursula swallowed. "Jimmy. Maybe you should go out." But he already had his jacket in his hand.

Jessica put her hand to her stomach as she saw her mother pulling out a letter from the envelope. "Oh, my God," she whispered. She clutched Ursula's arm.

They watched as Kate started to read the letter – then she covered her mouth, dropped to her knees in the snow, and clutched the letter to her breast, weeping.

Jessica broke down crying.

Tears shot to Ursula's eyes. "No! Please God, no."

She and Jessica rushed out to the porch and saw Jimmy run towards their mother and kneel down beside her. Kate grabbed his arm and handed him the letter.

He briefly scanned it, then jumped to his feet. "He's alive! He's alive!" He whooped and waved the letter at his sisters. "He's alive! Eugene's alive!" He lifted Kate up and squeezed her.

Both girls ran out in their stockinged feet, down the steps, down the lane, running to embrace their mother and Jimmy. Through blurry eyes they tried to read the letter for themselves.

Jimmy's face was wet with tears, though his smile couldn't be any wider. "I knew it! The son of a gun escaped them. No one is gonna get our Eugene!" He pointed to the letter. "Look! A broken arm, a few stitches in his leg. That's all! He's in a hospital being looked after by a pretty French nurse. What did I tell you! Didn't I tell you he'd be okay?"

Kate was still sobbing, but was smiling at Jimmy. "Yes, you did." She held the letter, read it again, and pressed it to her heart. "My boy! My darling boy. I knew he wouldn't leave me. I knew it."

Ursula and Jessica had their arms around her, tears running down their cheeks. Kate quickly shifted to protective mother, and made herself smile.

"Go inside, girls!" she said, laughing. "Look at you – no shoes. Oh my God!" She squeezed them all. "Eugene is alive! And well!"

They made their way to the house, with Jessica and Ursula on either side of their mother. Jimmy walked ahead of them, wiping his eyes, and saying again and again that no one was going to get Eugene or Paul.

"This calls for a real celebration!" said Jimmy. "We're all going into town tonight and I'm going to dance with my three best girls and we're all going to have a dance for ole Eugene! That son of a gun!"

"Then we'd better get dressed," Kate said, her face shining in euphoria. "The Bloomfields will be here any minute."

Ursula went to her room to dress, and collapsed on her bed in gratitude. She had begun to believe that Eugene had been killed, and was overwhelmed that she would once again see her eldest brother. While she dressed, she kept telling herself, Eugene is safe. That's all that matters. He's alive. Everything else will fall as it will.

She was afraid her dresses would be too snug, but she still fit into the blue satin dress she had worn to last year's dance. It was her favorite, and she felt a certain nostalgia for it. Friedrich had seen her in it before last year's dance, and he later told her he still carried that image of her in his mind: of her standing in the kitchen doorway, her eyes on him. Perhaps it would be the last time she would ever wear it.

She stood in front of the mirror and examined herself from different angles. Yes, she was a little fuller, but not enough for anyone to take notice. Still, she would wear her long cardigan over it. She wished that Friedrich could see her in it one last time, but Otto had finished up early with the POWs and taken them back to camp. She touched her amethyst earrings, remembering how Friedrich had so wanted to buy her the amethyst ring. One day, they would be married. One day, they would live together as a family.

Voices floated up the stairs, pulling her away from her visions. The Bloomfields had arrived, and by all the laughter and exclamations, they were hearing the good news about Eugene. Ursula put on her coat and went downstairs to join them.

In the kitchen, they decided who would go in which car. It was decided that Kate and Jessica would ride with the Bloomfields. Kate was suddenly eager to help Mrs. Bloomfield set up the dessert table.

"We'll be right behind you," said Jimmy. "I promised to bring the generator. Ed said Opal wanted it for the drinks. Last year all the ice melted."

"Why, I don't remember that," said Jessica. "Well, don't get your clothes dirty. Gladys won't want to dance with you. And we really can do without it, Jimmy. You're just making more work for everyone."

"Mind your own business," said Jimmy. "And why the heck are you carrying that bag around with you every time we go somewhere?"

"Emergency supplies for the dance," Jessica replied. "I have to be ready for any eventuality."

Ursula laughed at the sparring between them.

At the last minute, Sue Ellen decided to ride in the truck with Jimmy and Ursula. "I'll just squeeze in beside you, Ursula. Joe'll bring me home, but he doesn't want to get there too early. Imagine that! Let me get those!" she hollered to Kate, and ran to the porch to help with the pies.

"Dang!" Jimmy muttered.

"Shhh!" said Ursula. "She'll hear you. It's not like she'll slow us down."

"No, but her chattering might injure my head," he said, lifting the generator into the truck bed.

Ursula heard small groans coming from him on their way into town at Sue Ellen's minute descriptions of everything she had baked, including all the ingredients, exact measurements, and baking time. And how she asked Joe's opinion on each and every one of them, and his comments, and which ones she thought had turned out the best, compared to last year's, and how they had all agreed that it was her peach pie that was her best, and so she had made double the number so that no one would...

When he pulled up alongside the entrance to the hall, they saw that Kate was surrounded by a crowd of people and was sharing the news about Eugene. She looked ten years younger, vibrant and smiling. There was the mother they remembered.

They made their way inside, and while the women helped to set up the dessert table, Jimmy went from one group of people to another, looking for Gladys.

The crowd poured in while Sue Ellen and her mother worked on positioning their baked goods to advantage. Kate helped to calm the flustered Sue Ellen who couldn't find the pie servers, and assured several people that she would save them a slice of this pie or that cake. Jessica and Shirley were still giving directions on hanging the banner that pointed to the entrance.

Gladys soon appeared at their side. "Jimmy said you could use some help," she said.

"Why, thank you," Kate said, surprised that Jimmy would give up any of his time with Gladys.

More pies and cakes arrived and the table was soon full as Jessica came over to admire.

"Shirley asked Bob Rogers to help with the sign. That was my cue to leave."

Ursula smiled up at her from the table, and saw that Jimmy was talking to Otto, waving his arms, while Otto scratched his head. Then they left out the side door.

"We don't even need the stupid generator," said Jessica. "I told him that again and again. Now he's going to waste time going to get it fixed."

Kate laughed. "Let him be. You know how he likes to make sure that everything is in order. He'll be back soon to dance with Gladys here."

The hall filled up with people, men in uniform, families, and couples. Someone began to play Christmas music at the piano while the band set up.

Fifteen minutes later, Jessica saw Otto come back in the side door, but without Jimmy. She went to him and tugged on his arm. "Now where's Jimmy?"

"He's hell bent on getting that dang thing working. Had me go with him to the camp and insist that Friedrich fix the thing. Then just when we got back here, he drove off. Said he would get Burly to help them."

Jessica's eyes sharpened and she scanned the room for Ursula. There she was, listening politely to a group of older women, when Jimmy came back in and pulled her aside. He said something to her that caused her to look up with an expression of reluctance. He draped her coat over her shoulders, and pulled her outside.

Jessica gasped and hastened back to the dessert table, and reached underneath for the bag she'd brought with her. She grabbed her coat and hurried to catch up with Jimmy and Ursula. But by the time she made it through the crowd and to the door, they were already driving off. She ran to see the direction they were headed in. Her eyes narrowed. "I knew it!"

Ursula was annoyed with Jimmy, dragging her out into the cold. Rambling on about needing her help at Burly's shop while he fixed the generator.

"But it makes no sense, Jimmy," she said again. "Why didn't you just take Ed or Otto with you? What can I do?" She was distracted by his fidgety movements – checking and rechecking the rear-view mirror.

"For God's sake, Jimmy, what is it?"

He stopped the truck and faced her. "Get out and go to the church. Use the side door."

They stared at each other for several seconds. "Just do what I say. And make sure no one sees you. I'll be right there."

Ursula's eyes widened and her heart began to pound. She scrambled out of the truck and looked around, then turned down the alley and cut across to the side of the church.

Jimmy drove back to the machine shop. There was Friedrich, standing by the generator. He shook his head in confusion at Jimmy. "It works. There is nothing wrong with it."

"That's good," said Jimmy. He nodded to Burly. "Thanks for staying open. You can close up now and go to the dance."

"I'll help you with – "

"We can get it." He pointed his chin towards Friedrich. "I need to get this one back to camp. Thanks again, Burly. See you soon."

Friedrich helped him lift the generator back into the truck. "But I didn't do anything to it."

"Get in the truck. Hurry." Jimmy went around to the front and started the engine.

Friedrich got in, and sat silently as Jimmy wound his way around town, casting nervous glances about him. When the truck stopped behind a building, he shot a nervous glance to Jimmy.

"Get out!" said Jimmy, checking his mirrors and looking all around him.

A look of resignation filled Friedrich's face. He was ready to accept the punishment he deserved.

Jimmy came around and opened Friedrich's door, and read his expression. "Oh, for Christ's sake, will you just get out? Come on, hurry up!"

He took Friedrich by the arm, and pulled him towards the side door, then opened it and shoved him in.

"Friedrich!" Ursula cried, running to him.

Friedrich's mouth dropped open. He jerked his head from Ursula to the old German priest at the altar who was lighting the candles, and back to

Ursula's beaming face. In stunned amazement, he flashed on the meaning of it all.

Jimmy took a final look outside the door, and let out a breath of relief. "Now hurry up! Five minutes is gonna to have to do it."

Friedrich remained speechless and kept turning from Ursula to Jimmy.

Jimmy stood before them. "This will have to do for now. The paper part's gonna have to wait," he said. "In the eyes of God, and of each other, you two will be married. That's all that matters. For now." He pushed them up to the front, and then fished around in his pocket. He pulled out two gold bands and placed one in each of their palms. "Here."

Friedrich and Ursula stared at Jimmy in disbelief, and were about to speak, but Jimmy nodded to the priest. "Better get started." He took a few steps back and motioned for the ceremony to begin.

The priest began to say a few words in German, then in English, and Friedrich took Ursula by the hand and led her up to the altar.

After a few more words, they heard a sound at the side door, and saw the handle turn. A look of alarm filled their faces, and in an instant they envisioned a court-martial, prison, policemen…

Jimmy ran to prevent the door from opening. But was not in time.

The door was pushed open and Jessica stepped inside. "Aha! I thought so! Not without me, you don't."

Jimmy threw up his hands in exasperation. "Jessica! What the hell are *you* doing here?"

"The same thing you're doing." She made her way to the altar, clutching the little bag. She threw a look of indignation at Jimmy, that he dared undertake this without her.

Jimmy pulled at his hair and ran to the door. He poked his head around and tried to find a way to secure the door.

"Don't worry," said Jessica. "Everyone's at the dance."

"Jessica!" cried Ursula. "You shouldn't – "

"You are *not* getting married without a bridesmaid! And, as I am your sister, that would be me," she said sweetly, and nodded hello to the priest.

Jimmy groaned and spun around. "We're all going to be thrown in jail," he muttered. He turned to Ursula. "I thought you said no one else knew?"

"She just told me that she knew. I – "

The priest cleared his throat, as if perhaps all that could be sorted out later.

Jessica was pulling something from her bag. "And you cannot get married without a veil." She pulled out the ivory netting with the embroidered flowers.

Ursula watched wide-eyed, her mouth open, astonished to think that Jessica had calmly been making her bridal veil right under her nose.

Jessica draped it over her sister's hair, carefully arranging the folds around her face, and smiled at the effect. In the golden flicker of the candlelight, Ursula's earrings glittered and the ivory veil showed richly against her dark hair. For a moment, everyone was struck silent; Ursula's already stunning beauty was heightened to an unearthly love-liness.

Friedrich faced his bride and let out a gasp. "My Ursula – " he began, but could go no further. He was overwhelmed by her beauty, the love in her eyes, and that they were about to become husband and wife.

Jessica pulled out a bouquet of silk flow-ers and handed them to Ursula. "They're not real, but it is December, after all." She took a moment to arrange the flowers, and then lowered a bit of the veil over Ursula's face. Then she took off her coat and adjusted her dress, quite finished with the preparations.

Jimmy stood gaping, hands on his sides. "I suppose you got some champagne and glasses in there, as well?"

Jessica smiled at him and positioned herself next to Ursula. "Do we have a best man present?"

Jimmy rolled his eyes, and stepped up beside Friedrich. "That would be me," he said to the priest.

The priest continued with his service, in German and English. At the final words, Friedrich lifted the veil, his eyes shining. He kissed his wife, and then wrapped his arms around her. And Ursula embraced her husband, as if she was never letting go.

Jessica and Jimmy both smiled through their tears, though Jimmy kept brushing his away.

Friedrich took the old priest's hand, and spoke a few words of gratitude in German. Ursula also turned to the priest, and said softly, "*Danke schoen.*" The priest smiled and gave them a final blessing, and began to gather his things.

Ursula then went to Jimmy and held him tightly. "Jimmy! We will never forget this. Never!"

Jessica offered her hand to Friedrich, but he burst into a big smile and swooped down to hug her. Then he impulsively stepped over to Jimmy, taking him by surprise, and wrapped him in a bear hug. After a moment of astonishment, Jimmy gave in and hugged him back. Then he slapped him on the back, his smile as broad as Friedrich's.

Jimmy cleared his throat and tried to shift back to the logistics. "Well, I better get him back to camp before they start looking for him. Then I'll drive Father Hebenstreit to the train station. You two get back to the hall." He went to the side door and slowly opened it, looking around.

When Ursula and Jessica both rushed him with an embrace, he shook them off. "I'll be glad to get back on ship. You two girls are more dangerous than the Japs."

Before he could leave, Ursula and Friedrich embraced him one more time, thanking him again and again.

Jimmy wrapped his arms around them, and then took a step back. That was enough of teary-eyed emotions for him. He held up a threatening finger to them. "If it's a boy, his middle name better damned sure be James! Come on."

He and Jessica left with the priest, giving Friedrich and Ursula a moment alone together. Jimmy opened the door of the truck for the elderly priest and thanked him.

Jessica had repacked her little bag and now gave it to Jimmy. "Put this under the seat, will you?

Ursula and I will be missed at the hall. We'll say we stopped by to try to get Mrs. Kerry to come with us. Don't worry, I saw her arrive, just as I was leaving."

Jimmy shook his head. "I never knew you had it in you, Jess. Nerves of steel. Like all the women in our family. Me? My knees are still knocking." He kissed her cheek. "You did good, Jess. I'll see you soon."

Ursula and Friedrich came out of the church, transformed. Happy, full of future, their love forever sealed.

"Come," said Jessica to Ursula, taking her by the arm. "Let's not press our luck. We'll save you a dance, Jimmy!" she hollered over her shoulder. The two sisters hurried off, arm in arm, laughing in joy, turning around just as the truck rounded the corner and headed back to camp.

Chapter 17

Charles called home each of the three days he was gone. On the last night, he called to say he would be home the following day. He would have two days at home, before flying out on the 23rd. His calls seemed to help the boys adjust. Instead of moping, they were excited that he would be home again.

Time enough for a hasty goodbye, thought Lillian. Though it was so much less than she had expected, and it meant no trip to Annette's and no anniversary celebration, she would at least hold him in her arms again.

She spent all day preparing for his arrival, using up the last of her sugar to bake a pecan pie. But surprisingly, the boys were being difficult about the meal she was planning for that evening.

"Why do you keep looking out the window?" she asked them.

"Mickey and Billy are going to stop by," said Tommy. "They want us to go to the diner with them."

"The diner? Your father will be home soon and he'll expect you to be here. I baked a casserole and a pie especially for tonight."

"Oh – we thought it was tomorrow," said Tommy, cracking his knuckles.

"Maybe Dad would like to go to the diner with us," suggested Gabriel. He looked at Tommy, and Lillian saw Tommy give a quick shake of his head.

"You boys have been behaving mysteriously all day." She turned around to look at them more carefully. "Look at you, all dressed to go out. What's going on with you two?"

"We just want to look nice for Dad," said Tommy.

"You just said you thought he wasn't coming – Oh, never mind." Lillian shook her head, and glanced at the clock. Then she put the casserole in the oven to bake.

Tommy and Gabriel were looking out the window, whispering.

"Don't worry, boys. He's on his way. He'll be here in time for dinner." She took off her apron. "I've been cooking all day. I'm just going to wash up a bit. Keep your eye on the casserole for me, will you?"

"Sure, Mom," said Tommy.

She looked from Tommy to Gabriel. Gabriel gave her a wide smile and stayed smiling for no apparent reason until Tommy nudged him.

Again, she shook her head. She took a quick bath and tried to think of how she could make the most of the next two days. She dressed carefully, putting on a good dress, and added a dab of perfume, a touch of lipstick. She was determined to make it a special evening, even though it would be a simple meal and some time together at home.

When she came out into the kitchen, she saw that the oven had been shut off and the casserole put back in the refrigerator.

"Tommy! This should have been in the oven half an hour ago!" She glanced at the clock. "Why did you take it out?"

Tommy stood staring at her.

"We were afraid it would burn," said Gabriel.

"Yeah," said Tommy. "We thought we should wait until Dad gets here."

She turned on the oven again, and placed the casserole back inside, banging the door shut. "Now it won't be done in time! Since when did you boys start making decisions about cooking?"

But their eyes were glued to the window, and they didn't answer her. They craned their necks to look up the street.

"There's Dad!" they both cried. "Mom, Dad is here!"

"And now dinner will be late!" she said in exasperation.

The boys ran to the door, and then down the stairs. Lillian waited at the door.

Soon they all entered and Lillian embraced Charles. The boys were giddy with excitement, running to the kitchen and back to the door.

"Wonderful news!" Charles said, wrapping his arms around Lillian. "I was granted an extra day!" He winked at the boys, and put an arm around their shoulders.

"Sit down, Charles. Let me pour you a glass of wine." When she went into the kitchen, she saw that the oven had been shut off again. She whipped around with her hands on her hips. "Thomas Drooms!" She saw that Gabriel was trying not to laugh.

Just then the buzzer rang, and Tommy and Gabriel ran down the stairs.

"Tommy! Gabriel!" She turned in perplexity to Charles. "They got it into their heads that they want to go to the diner. I don't know what's got into them." She heard the vestibule door close, and then laughter and running footsteps. "They've been behaving oddly all day, whispering, and – " She stopped mid-sentence when Izzy appeared at the door, escorted by Tommy and Gabriel.

"Izzy!" Lillian tucked her chin in surprise, and then looked from Izzy to the boys to Charles. "Will someone please tell me what's going on?"

Charles swept her off her feet and kissed her cheek, causing the boys and Izzy to laugh.

"Charles! For heaven's sake, put me down! What's going on?"

"You better tell her before she bursts," Izzy said.

Charles set her down, but kept his arms tightly around her. "We're going to celebrate our anniversary tonight."

Lillian started to speak but he continued.

"I have it all planned – with a little help," he added, smiling at the boys and Izzy. "Why don't you go pack your bag?"

"My bag? Are we going somewhere?"

"Someplace close. But make sure to pack your green dress."

"My green dress?" Her eyes began to tear up, but then she broke into a smile. "And you all knew about this?" she asked, in mock offense.

"Yep," said Izzy. "I'm spending the night here tonight. And the boys and I have a busy evening planned. The diner, a movie, and late-night dessert at Buttercup's."

Lillian pinched Tommy and Gabriel's cheeks. "Fooling your poor mother," she said with a laugh.

Izzy took her arm. "Come on, I'll help you pack. You need to hurry. Your carriage is waiting. And that took some finagling, let me tell you."

Lillian didn't understand what she was getting at until ten minutes later when they all rushed downstairs and she saw that there was indeed a Central Park horse and carriage waiting for them.

Amid the most cheerful goodbyes she ever heard, Lillian let Charles help her into the carriage and they crossed into Central Park.

And there began the most wonderful evening Lillian had ever known. The slow drive through the snow-covered park was itself a high point, but when the carriage ended up at The Plaza Hotel, the evening grew in its magic.

"Charles! You remembered!" Again, tears shot to her eyes to think that Charles had not forgotten her old wish.

Their room overlooked the park, just as she had always dreamed. The evening was full of dinner and dancing, with Lillian wearing the dress she had worn the first time she went out with Charles, the emerald satin shot through with iridescent blue.

Over dinner, Charles presented her with the Victorian sapphire ring, and looked at her with love. "Happy anniversary, my darling."

"Charles!" she said, slipping it on her finger. "It's beautiful."

He took her hands and kissed them. "You are everything to me, Lillian. My life with you and the boys is more than anything I ever could have dreamed of."

"For me, too, Charles. My life couldn't be more complete. I have everything. Everything. I only want more of it."

"That will come. Once this war is over, we will have a beautiful life."

A night of closeness followed, and in the dark hours of early morning, Lillian awoke, still feeling that she was inhabiting a dream. She woke with the curious sensation of being absolutely, one hundred percent certain that she had conceived. She sat up in bed, and then walked to the window, and parted the curtains. She gazed down at the lamplights dotting the park, and then back at her husband, thinking, *What a wondrous, mysterious, beautiful thing is life!*

"Charles!" she said softly, wanting to tell him her news.

"Hmm?" came his sleepy voice.

She smoothed down the front of her negligee, and smiled, telling herself she couldn't possibly know such a thing – and yet she was sure. She slid into the warm bed, kissed his cheek, and spoke softly: "Merry Christmas, my darling."

Made in the USA
Monee, IL
29 December 2023